His Christmas Miracle

His Christmas Miracle

Dani Collins

His Christmas Miracle
Copyright © 2016 Dani Collins
Tule Publishing First Printing, August 2016

The Tule Publishing Group, LLC

ALL RIGHTS RESERVED

No part of this book may be used or reproduced in any manner whatsoever without written permission except in the case of brief quotations embodied in critical articles and reviews.

This is a work of fiction. Names, characters, places, and incidents are products of the author's imagination or are used fictitiously. Any resemblance to actual events, locales, organizations, or persons, living or dead, is entirely coincidental.

ISBN: 978-1-945879-21-0

Dedication

To you, my wonderful fans. I am grateful and humbled by your continued support. May you be blessed with a miracle of your own. Much love, Dani.

Dear Reader,

Writing a Christmas book is a lot like Christmas itself. You have so many wonderful elements to draw on to make for memorable moments.

As I brainstormed this one, I began listing fun winter activities like sleigh rides and baking cookies, building a gingerbread house and, of course, visiting the increasingly famous Marietta Stroll. Pretty soon I was wondering how I would fit it all in and started mapping it on a calendar, trying to figure out the timing and… Wait a minute.

Some years ago, when my children were still young, I was visiting a friend in December. I saw she had made a home-made advent calendar for her children. I had only ever seen the chocolate kind. She told me she filled hers with 'chachkies.' Trinkets.

The memory came back to me as I was writing this book. You'll see that Nicki had one like my friend's, but when Nicki makes one for Atlas, she takes it in yet another direction. Recognizing that Quincy needs to bond with his son, she plans a Christmas themed activity for each day through December. At first, Quincy is *not* impressed, but soon he's checking the calendar to see what's next.

I had a lot of fun with this and thought you might, too. I am *thrilled* to include a special bonus with this book. Look for a link at the end of this book to download a printable advent calendar similar to the one Nicki makes. It includes instructions for a few simple crafts, some popular recipes, and a list of suggested activities to make your own countdown to Christmas memorable.

Have a wonderful Christmas and a happy New Year!
Dani

November 30th

NICOLE DARREN PULLED her hatchback into the address on the outskirts of Marietta and let out a relieved breath. That drive through icy passes and swirling snowflakes had been a nightmare—and she had splurged on *good* snow tires.

Well, she had spent her father's money on them, but she wouldn't have arrived in one piece if she hadn't. And she was going to pay him back.

Right after she landed this job.

With another cleansing breath, she tugged her hat onto her head, pulling hard enough to bring the pink-and-yellow tails under her chin, then tied them off. As she stepped outside, her nose pinched and her eyes watered, stung by the fierce, biting wind.

I missed you, too, Montana. Ugh. Maybe she should have waited until May to leave California.

After slamming her car door, she pocketed her keys, then zipped her consignment-store ski jacket, taking in the farmhouse as she started toward it. It was two stories with a single-story addition wrapped in a covered porch off to the left. The east side, maybe? She was terrible with directions, but she knew pretty when she saw it.

In the waning light of afternoon, surrounded by the blowing snow, the house looked surprisingly sweet. It was in good repair, obviously restored by loving hands that had a flair for "quaint". She adored the bold eggplant with teal trim and yellow rails. On a sunny day, it would be bright and welcoming, making any passerby smile. There was even an old washtub next to the stairs, sleeping under a layer of snow, but with a few ice-coated, brown stalks poking through, promising to greet visitors with a riot of blooms come spring.

Delighted by the idea of working for someone with such a warm, artistic bend, she clomped up the steps, rang the bell, then looked for a broom to sweep her footprints.

The door opened and a man was backlit through the screen. She saw more silhouette than expression. He was tall and had wide, strapping shoulders beneath a white-and-blue striped button shirt. No hat, cowboy or otherwise. He wore a neatly trimmed beard the same color as his dark brown hair.

He did *not* look like he needed a nursing aide.

She smiled as if he were her new boss. "Am I at the right house? Are you Ryan Quincy? I'm Nicki Darren."

"Quincy Ryan." He started to push the screen toward her.

"I'm sorry." She stepped back, then loosened her boots

and stepped out of them, leaving them on the welcome mat as she entered. "I thought the recruitment site got it backward, and Ryan was your first name."

"That happens a lot." He didn't smile. In fact, he was doing a great imitation of the arctic outflow wind that he locked outside as he closed the door behind her.

Now she was in the foyer and could properly see him, she realized he was really good looking. Her inner spinster warmed and fanned herself. The aspiring actress who had been around that many pretty boys for the last seven years said, *Oh, please.*

But he was *really* good looking. He was a head taller than she was, fit and trim with dark brown eyes, brows that were on the stern side, and a jaw that was wide enough to be strong. It was beautifully framed with stubble grown just long enough to make her want to touch his cheek, suspecting it was smooth, not scratchy. He was one of those quietly powerful types of men who were natural leaders because people couldn't help but look up and defer to him.

At the same time, he gave off such an attitude of aloof superiority, she had to catch back an exasperated chuckle. She had left L.A. precisely to distance herself from this sort of arrogance, and to get back to being around real people who were nice to one another because it was the decent way to behave.

Do. Not. Blow. This.

"You have a beautiful home." Compliments were always

a good start, right? She tugged off her hat and flashed another friendly grin at him. Maybe her face hadn't opened as many doors as she would have liked, but her smile usually prompted an answering one when she offered it.

"It's not mine. My father grew up here and just bought it again. We had nothing to do with this."

The jerk of his head disparaged the crown molding, the polished hardwood floors, and the glossy white wainscoting under cornflower-blue wallpaper with white polka dots. Each of the stair treads was carpeted in blue while the risers were painted white. She would bet any money the kitchen was buttercup yellow.

"I see." She didn't. She instantly loved everything about this house and wanted to tell him how lucky he was. She'd been sharing rooms with cockroaches and starving actors. She hadn't had her own space in years, let alone anything so dollhouse perfect.

"I just drove in from California. That was a shock to the system." She thumbed toward the window draped in white curtains held open with bands of blue. Outside, flakes continued to swirl in the dusk.

"It was like this in Philly. And all the way across." He frowned as he led her into a living room where the furniture was off center on its area rug. Boxes were stacked against the wall. In the empty, adjoining dining room, a gray modular desk was coming together, a handful of pieces still wrapped in shrink film. "We got in late last night. I thought your resume showed a Montana address?"

"My father's place. One way or another, I was giving up my room in L.A. Since Glacier Creek is where I was born…" She shrugged as she removed her jacket and draped it across her thighs as she lowered to perch on the sofa across from him. "It's where I'm headed if I don't take a job elsewhere."

She tried to make it sound like she had options other than this one.

He took the wingback, seeming to weigh her words. Did he think she was dishonest? Misrepresenting? Her palms began to sweat. She needed this job *so bad*.

A laptop stood open on the coffee table. Thankfully, there was only one file folder beside it, with her name on it.

Don't send me crawling back to Glacier Creek. Please.

She had left anything that didn't fit in her hatchback in California, then had barely slept in Utah, afraid her few remaining possessions would be stolen overnight, even though the couple she had found through a B&B app had assured her their neighborhood was very safe. She hadn't detoured to stay with her father and stepmother on her way here either. Telling them she was back in Montana could wait until she had aced this interview. That was what she kept telling herself.

If she didn't get the job, well, she could already hear her stepmother, Gloria, saying, "*I told you so*."

"You didn't list previous experience." Quincy Ryan lifted his gaze from studying her file. He sounded skeptical.

Looked dubious.

"I completed my certification earlier this year and did a practicum at an assisted-living home in Santa Monica. I was able to stay on at the facility a few extra months to cover for someone on leave. I've been working in the field all this time."

She had to force herself not to blurt the words out too fast, but she was anxious to impress on him that she wasn't completely green. Squishing her palms together between her knees, she fought to keep her voice measured and warm.

"But the cost of living in California is, well, prohibitive. And I was ready for a change. Montana always felt like home, so when I saw this position, I was really excited. I love the idea of being back here."

Too much enthusiasm? She didn't know how to read that blank stare of his and kept getting distracted by the stark beauty of his sculpted features.

He dropped his attention back to the folder. "No experience with children, either."

"Well, babysitting, of course. When I was a teenager." Everyone had that, didn't they? "I also have CPR and the first aid that was part of my training. Plus, I took an elective certificate on diet and nutrition, so I can prepare meals along with, you know, spoon-feeding if he isn't feeding himself. But I understood from the posting that the boy is four and there were no specific health concerns. Is that right?"

His lips went tight. He kept his gaze on the open file

folder in his hand. "Yes."

"But there's a senior who is diabetic?"

"My father. Yes. He has an insulin pump and takes blood pressure medication. If it were only him, I could monitor that myself, but with Atlas… It's too much to ask my father to watch him all day, and I have to work." His gaze came up, flat and unreadable. "The position is more nanny than nurse. Full days of child minding and housekeeping, cooking and laundry. Whatever they both need, every day until Christmas. Preschool starts in January. I have someone arranged to help out then."

Whatever *they* need, not him. Something about that struck her, but she was concentrating more on keeping her hand from waving wildly in the air as the words, *Pick me*, crowded her throat. She didn't care if it was only for a few weeks. She needed the money.

"Atlas is your son?"

"Yes." He didn't say it with as much conviction as she would have expected.

"And you're not married?" She wasn't being sexist, assuming his wife would take care of everyone, but he hadn't mentioned a spouse.

"His mother and I weren't together. She passed away last month. Car accident."

"Oh." *Wow.* She had a lot of questions about each of those bullet-point statements, but she was overcome with such a wave of empathy for little Atlas, her chest grew tight.

"I'm so sorry," she said with deep sincerity. "I lost my mom when I was eleven. He must be having a very rough time." Her eyes welled before she could even try to stop it, old loss hitting afresh. And it was coming up to Christmas, too.

She looked around for the tike, wanting to hug him. That was all she had wanted when she'd been in his shoes—for someone to hug her. A little love went a long way when your world had completely shattered.

"I, uh…" Quincy did the man-panic and quickly stood to snatch a box of tissues from where it poked from an open box. He offered it to her. "Here."

"I'm sorry. I'm fine," she hurried to insist, forcing an abashed smile as she quickly dabbed and pulled herself together. How to *not* make a great first impression. *Sheesh*.

It struck her that Quincy had only mentioned his father. "Your mother isn't with you?"

"Gone twelve years." His face spasmed very briefly, the first sign of emotion she'd seen in him. "Cancer. Hit me hard at twenty. I can't imagine at four." He didn't look at her, only seemed to take great care centering her single-sheet resume in the crease of the folder.

"I'm so sorry." She meant it.

Quincy lifted his gaze. They sat in the shadow of grief for two slow heartbeats while the disquiet in his expression eased.

Then, as if he remembered they were strangers, he quickly re-enshrined his thoughts and feelings into their tomb. He glanced away. When his gaze came back, it was cool and unreadable.

"What were you doing before taking your certification?" It seemed a deliberate change of topic.

"Deluding myself." She went for good-natured self-deprecation to hide the fact she wanted to shrivel into a ball every time she confronted her spectacular failure in California. *See, Gloria? I can act.*

Quincy's brows went up.

"I, uh, had aspirations to star in movies. Apparently, so does the rest of Montana and every other state besides." She scratched her brow, shrugging off years of heartbreak and struggle as if they were inconsequential. They were. No one cared. Only her. "You can only survive on ramen noodles for so long, right? I was flat out told I was getting too old. I'm twenty-*five*."

She still couldn't believe those words had been spoken to her and railed on with the subdued outrage she'd been trying to exorcise since it happened.

"My agent said she was cutting her list down to people under twenty. She only wanted talent who had the potential to pay back the investment of her time. Basically, she was saying even if I landed a good part tomorrow, I was already over the hill. My chances of building a career had passed. Isn't that horrible? I was already tired of living hand to mouth, but still."

She had fought against giving up. She had fought against accepting reality, so Gloria wouldn't be right.

She sighed, still blue, but determined to believe the universe had a plan. "What she said got me thinking, though. About people who are *actually* in their golden years and dismissed by society. I looked into jobs in nursing homes. Then, when I actually started volunteering with seniors... I didn't realize how depressed I was from all those years of rejection."

Her heart lightened just thinking about those early days. She'd wondered if she was being punked, she'd been so astonished by the change in attitude.

"People were happy to see me and eager to chat. They thanked me for the smallest things. Like taking their blood pressure or pouring a glass of water. It's my job. Why would I need thanks for that? But it made me feel so good. *Such* a nice change. And I remembered that people used to be friendly and sincere back home, so I decided to move back here. I'm over-sharing, aren't I?"

She halted as she realized how badly she was running on. Dear Lord, the man was a robot. Stare, stare, stare, like he was cataloguing her brain with his laser vision.

"I'm just saying that it feels good to do something that helps people. I took the training so I would have marketable qualifications and more opportunity, but I'm eager to work wherever and however I'm needed. That's why I applied for this job, even though it's temporary and involves more childcare than senior care."

Even if it would only allow her to pay her father back for the tires when she saw him at Christmas. The ledger sheet between her and her father was heavily in the red on her side. *Please* let her start balancing it out and prove she was amounting to something.

"So…" She swallowed, unable to stand the suspense. "What do you think?"

HE THOUGHT SHE was a parakeet.

Par for the course, Quincy supposed, since he was residing in a house colored up like a peacock.

He used his thumbnail to scratch the line of his beard at the corner of his jaw, then turned over the single sheet in the folder he held. Surprise, surprise, very few people wanted to relocate to map-speck Montana for the month of December. The woman he'd hired briefly in Philly hadn't wanted anything to do with such a big move to such a small place for such a short time.

Quincy had made inquiries here in Marietta a few months ago, when Pops had first announced his intention to move back here. At that time, he had only needed someone willing to look in once a day. His father was quite capable of living on his own, but things were different now.

So different.

Still, it was only one month. Three weeks, really. Once

Atlas was in the all-day preschool, Quincy figured he could handle most of the daily stuff. *Other parents did.* At that point, they could settle for having a housekeeper come in once or twice a week.

He just needed help through December, while they got settled and he finished up some work projects.

He needed time to get used to all of this.

But he wasn't even given time to decide if he should introduce her to his father. The swing door near the bottom of the stairs squeaked. Pops and Atlas came through from the kitchen.

"Oh. I didn't realize we had company." Pops redirected Atlas from the bottom of the stairs into the living room. "We were going to find a clean shirt, but hello."

"Hello." Nicki Darren stood.

Pops was carrying too much weight, which contributed to the diabetes, but he came forward with enthusiasm.

"Maurice Ryan. Call me Maury."

"Nicki." She shook his hand and offered a big smile.

House, meet fire. His father had spent most of his life in sales and got along with everyone. Quincy had already noted that Ms. Darren didn't exactly hold back, either. They quickly covered the weather, driving conditions, and the 'excitement' of a big move.

Atlas hung back, his blue shirt stained with a few dribbles of tomato soup. The battered stuffed dog he liked to cart around hung from his grip.

"*You have a son,*" the lawyer had said, after asking if Quincy had once dated Karen Ackerman.

"*Five years ago,*" he replied. He didn't like to talk about it because he still felt blindsided by the entire thing. After they met online, things had progressed more quickly than he had expected. He had thought that meant they were serious and started looking for rings.

They had burned out just as fast—on her side, anyway. He hadn't understood the break up. It had been a slap when he thought things were going well.

They definitely didn't have a son, though.

They hadn't, maybe, but *she* had.

"*He's staying with his maternal grandparents,*" the lawyer said. "*But you're identified as the father on his birth certificate. No one else has been designated for custody.*"

One paternity test later, Quincy knew his Y chromosome had created this boy, but being a biological father hadn't made him feel like a dad. He didn't know how to be a parent.

That hadn't mattered to Karen's parents. They were finished raising their own children. They hadn't approved of their adopted daughter having a child out of wedlock and keeping Quincy in the dark about him. They had not only insisted he be informed, but that he take responsibility.

Quincy privately believed they were holding him to account for something he hadn't even known he'd done.

He had been sleepwalking ever since. This wasn't real.

How could it be?

Now he was trying to hire some help and his best shot was a failed actress. Nicki Darren was way too freshly minted with her 'new' career to take this job seriously.

He started to cut short the conversation before Pops took too much for granted, but Pops was already drawing Atlas forward.

"And this is Atlas."

Pops was so proud to have a grandson, so *taken* with him. Quincy had gone to his father with the news the moment he'd hung up from the lawyer. Where else would he go with a shocker like that? He hadn't known what to do, how to react.

His father had stared at him as if he couldn't believe he had to spell it out for him. *"You take him and raise him, son."*

Quincy was damned grateful he had his father, a man who knew the ropes of parenting, since he didn't have a clue what to do with a boy that age himself. On the other hand, his father's reaction put so much pressure on him. *Love him*, Pops seemed to urge relentlessly.

How? Quincy could barely stand himself, let alone anyone else. His father was the only person he would admit—internally, mind you, and without any flowery language—that he loved outright. He couldn't simply look into a pair of brown eyes that yes, were disconcertingly similar to the ones he saw in the mirror every day, and fall in love. It was narcissistic, for starters.

He wasn't dad material. He had never intended to become one. Karen had known that. Which put another wrinkle of confusion into how this had come about.

"Hello, Atlas." Nicki knelt in front of him and shot a quick glance up at Quincy. "You look just like your father."

A jolt went through Quincy each time he met her gaze. The *zing* carried the adolescent *pow* of electric excitement that used to happen when the head cheerleader tossed a surprise smile at the trig nerd he'd been.

He definitely couldn't hire her. She was way too pretty. Pretty enough to be an actress, for sure, and definitely too pretty to be a nurse. She was noisy, too. Not just chatty, but he could already tell her personality was loud. She had been wearing a tacky hat when she first came in, a knitted pink-and-yellow thing with a big yellow pom-pom and earflaps that had trailed down into a pair of Technicolor Pocahontas braids.

She had popped it off and rich brown waves had tumbled around her face, hints of caramel and dark coffee giving the mass some depth. Fine strands had lifted with static and she had smiled so big his stomach had tightened with male reaction.

Now her jacket was on the sofa, allowing him to take in the snug pink turtleneck she wore. Her chest was as perfect as a woman could be made. Little glints of dark bronze caught the light as her hair shifted around her shoulders. Her hips flared above narrow thighs encased in skinny jeans. Her face had a sun-kissed California tone, or maybe she had some *Latina* heritage that gave her that soft glow. She wasn't wearing makeup and didn't need it. Those blackstrap molasses eyes of hers were sticky enough, practically gluing his gaze to her features, mesmerizing him.

Maybe he was using her as an excuse not to look at his son.

Son, son, son. He had to get over the shock and deal with it. He knew he did. But how? Hiring this woman couldn't be the answer. He needed a miracle.

"It sounds like a lot of things have changed for you lately," Nicki was saying to the boy. "Does it feel strange to be in a new house?"

Atlas brought the stuffed dog up to his chest and hugged it close. His expression grew even more shy than it usually was.

Who named a kid Atlas? He was a boy, not a titan. It made Quincy think the kid was being forced to carry too much. Damn it, if he could only have five minutes with Karen to ask how she'd become pregnant. *Why?*

He watched Atlas shift his little eyeballs up and down, between Nicki and him, weighing. Like he knew Quincy was making a decision that would affect him.

He'd been giving Quincy that same look since his grandparents had said, "*This is your father. You'll be living with him now.*"

Quincy probably wore one just like it. He hated change,

too, and always wanted some kind of warning.

"I'm Nicki." She offered her hand. "Nice to meet you." After a second, she said, "You're supposed to shake my hand."

Atlas did, gingerly.

"Good job." Nicki's voice held a warmth that made Quincy uncomfortable. It eased the tension in him a few notches. He needed resistance against her, not reassurance. He didn't know why, but he did.

The barest hint of a smile touched Atlas's mouth. Apparently, he wasn't immune to her star power either.

"I'm excited for Christmas. Are you?"

Atlas shrugged his bony shoulder.

Quincy bit back a groan. He didn't care about the holiday one way or another. After his mother had passed, he and his father always spent the day together, exchanging a gift of game tickets or hand tools and going out for a decent meal, but that was as far as either of their investment in celebrating went.

This year, Pops seemed to think it all had to be a big hoopla. Atlas didn't even know his days of the week, as far as Quincy could tell. Did he even understand what Christmas was, let alone why he should be counting days in anticipation?

"My favorite part is making cookies and decorating them. What do you like to do?"

"Pops is diabetic," Quincy reminded her.

His father shot him a look that told him to ease up, knotting Quincy's shoulders even further.

"I would love for this house to be full of the smell of ginger snaps and shortbread. My wife used to make them this time of year. So did my mother, come to think of it."

Nicki rose. "Quincy said you grew up here."

"I did. I left to make my fortune, as young men do, but I've always missed Marietta. When I saw the house had been restored and was for sale, I decided to buy it and move back. That was before we knew about Atlas. I thought I'd be living here alone. Now I have both my boys with me."

Quincy saw Nicki Darren's expression sharpen with curiosity, but Pops didn't give her a chance to ask what he meant by, *Before we knew.*

"We'll have to get a tree," Pops said. "You'll have to take us shopping, help us with the wrapping. Are you up to all of that?"

"Of course. Does that mean…?" Nicki clasped her hands under her chin. "Do I have the job?" She seemed to have more teeth than normal people. They were straight, pearly, and couldn't stand not to be seen because there they were *again.*

"Pops—"

"What? Did I get that wrong? I thought you were hiring her?"

"There's a lot of unpacking still to finish," Quincy warned her. "I have to work. That's why we need someone to…" He nodded at Atlas.

I don't know what to do with him.

In his periphery, he saw his father's chest rise and fall in subtle disappointment. It hit Quincy hard, every single time.

"If you're up to that, fine." Desperate times called for desperate measures. Maybe, given what she'd said about her own mom, and how she'd grown so sad and wistful mentioning it, maybe she understood where Atlas was at and could help the boy settle in. "Start as soon as you can. I need to finish building my desk."

He went back to the living room.

December 1st

DESPITE THREE DAYS of driving across the country, Quincy's body clock was still on East Coast time. He was up at five and fine with it. Better to get something done before—

Was that the toilet flushing? Pops?

He finished pulling on his T-shirt and sweats and opened his bedroom door, catching Atlas standing at the top of the stairs, peering through the uprights in the rail, down into the dark.

Atlas glanced back at him and shrank a little, like he thought he was in trouble.

Quincy wasn't used to looking out for anyone but himself. As far as being intuitive, reading body language and other subtle social cues, he had always been a little on the slow side. Math and structure were his bailiwick.

But since his own stomach was growling, Quincy had an idea what Atlas was looking for.

"Are you hungry? Do you want some breakfast?"

Atlas's nod was barely perceptible. He wore blue-and-red

pajamas with a superhero emblem on the chest. Quincy hadn't really taken stock of what Karen's parents had packed for the kid, but the pajamas were tight and showed his ankles and wrists. His feet were bare, one stacked on the other while his toes curled. He looked expectantly up at Quincy, making Quincy even more aware of the void in his stockpile of life skills.

How did you take care of someone else, especially a child?

"Are you cold? Do you have a robe? Slippers?"

Atlas shook his head.

"Put on socks then. And a sweater." He would turn up the heat, but it would take a while for the house to warm up.

Atlas scooted back to his room. Quincy fetched his own plaid, shrugging it on and returning to the top of the stairs.

As he stood there, he could see Atlas sitting on the floor of his bedroom, working a pair of socks onto his feet. It was a bit of a process. Quincy almost went in to help, but he held back. He just wasn't sure.

He *hated* not being sure. Once he'd found his confidence in work and his handful of social relationships, he had stuck to his lane until it was rock solid. Now he was slogging around in uneven terrain, tripping and stumbling with every step. It was a horrible feeling.

Atlas tugged on the pullover he'd been wearing yesterday, the one stained with soup. His head popped through and his fine brown hair stuck up with static as he walked toward the door.

It made Quincy think of rubbing a balloon on his head as a kid, trying to make his own hair stand on end. Maybe he smiled at the memory because Atlas's mouth pulled in a very quick, very tentative little smile.

At that moment, Pops let out a giant snore behind his bedroom door across the hall, startling them both.

Atlas's eyes widened, and Quincy found himself chuckling.

"It's easier to sleep when we're not sharing a room with that, isn't it?" Quincy was referring to the hotel rooms from their cross-country trip, but Atlas only gave him a wary look and started down the stairs, looking back at Pops' door like he was afraid another dinosaur noise would emerge.

Quincy bit back a sigh. He was *not* used to being the one to carry a conversation. On the flip side, if he'd had any doubts that Atlas was his son, the kid's reticence pretty much clinched it.

In the kitchen, which was a painfully cheerful yellow with white Shaker cupboards and a backsplash in robin's egg blue, Quincy set out the boxes of cereal he'd grabbed on a quick grocery run when they'd arrived in town.

"Which one do you like?" They were all adult and boring, Quincy realized. Not that he should feed a kid chocolate and marshmallows first thing, but maybe something with raisins?

He reached to start a grocery list and saw Nicki had already written 'supplies for cookies' and 'xmas lights' on the little pad of sticky notes. She had stuck around quite a while yesterday, unpacking Atlas's room and cooking breakfast for dinner. She had eaten with Pops and Atlas while Quincy had brought his own into the dining room where he was assembling his new desk.

Her handwriting was the opposite of his own. Hers was cursive and feminine, slanting this way and that, not quite closing her Os, and she crossed her T well after the upright line. Quincy added 'cereal' with the precision of the draftsman he was. Then added slippers, robe, and pajamas.

Atlas picked a flavor.

Quincy poured two bowls, then sat across from the boy to eat. *Crunch, munch, crunch. Clink. Slurp. Munch.*

Don't talk my ear off, kid.

"Listen." Quincy felt like an idiot having an adult conversation with a boy this young, but he had to get it off his chest. He realized with a start this was the first time he'd been alone with the boy. He'd been keeping Pops as close as Atlas kept his toy dog.

"I, uh, didn't know I had a son. That's why I didn't come to see you before. Before you had to go live with your granny and gramps, I mean."

Karen's parents had said Karen wanted to be a single mother. He knew she'd been adopted, but she had told *him* she didn't want kids. That was how they'd been matched by the online site.

Had she targeted him deliberately? Had her plan been to find herself an unwitting donor? Not a conversation he had wanted to have with her parents while they were grieving, but that was the impression he formed from the few details they had volunteered.

He frowned into his cereal.

Maybe she'd accidentally turned up pregnant and made the choice not to tell him. Maybe she simply hadn't wanted the complication of a man in her life.

Maybe she hadn't wanted *him*.

He cleared his throat. "I know this is strange. It's hard for both of us, but I'm sure we'll get to know each other. I didn't know Pops when I first met him, but we get along great now."

The joke was lost on the kid. Atlas only finished chewing, then licked the milk from his lips and finally spoke directly to Quincy for the very first time.

"When is Nicki comin' back?"

NICKI HAD STAYED at the house until seven last night, putting away Atlas's clothes and noting that his collection of toys was sparse.

Christmas was coming, though, and it sounded like Maury intended to be generous.

She didn't remember her own grandparents very well. They had passed when she'd been quite young. She hoped

Atlas had Maury for a long time. The older man was obviously eager to dote on him.

Which was great since Quincy seemed rather withdrawn. He'd said he and Atlas's mother weren't together, and she'd caught that strange comment from Maury.

Before we knew about Atlas.

He couldn't mean that Quincy had only discovered he had a son when Atlas's mother had died, could he? It would explain why he was so closed off and distant—from everything, it seemed. The move. His son.

She got the impression he was turned off and tuned out. Maybe he was still upset about Atlas's mom's death, too.

Whatever the reason, the dynamic was off. It made her feel for the boy all the more. As ill equipped as her father had been to console her, at least she'd stayed in her old bedroom and saw her friends at school every day.

Poor Atlas. His entire life had been shaken up like a snow globe. Things were only now starting to settle and allow him to see the picture again.

After a bath and getting him into his pajamas, she had sat on his bed with him to read a story. He'd fallen asleep halfway through, but as she had started to leave the bed, he had jerked awake and tried to hang onto her, only letting go as he realized she wasn't his mom.

He had welled up and she had gathered him into her lap where she had held him and rocked him, heart breaking into a thousand pieces as he sobbed inconsolably against her.

"I know, little man," she had crooned, rubbing his back, transported to the endless nights when she had cried alone in her own bed. "I know you miss her. It will be okay. I promise you."

It was a lie. She had never been *okay* with the loss of her mother, but she had learned to live with the absence. When the grief had been fresh, however, she had needed hope and hadn't had any.

She didn't want Atlas to feel the way she had—as though she'd been left abandoned in a big, awful world.

When he calmed, she said, "I'll lie here until you fall asleep. Then I'll be back in the morning. I *promise*. And we'll make cookies. I want you to think about how much fun we're going to have."

She was anxious to get back to him after all those vows, but she had to wait for the grocery store to open. A cursory look in the Ryan cupboards had found them wanting of a lot, especially the essentials like flour and baking powder.

While she waited, Nicki finished settling into her small bachelor apartment above the garage of friends of a friend.

When the interview for a job in Marietta had come up, Nicki had put out a call on social media, asking if anyone could hook her up with accommodation on short notice. Her schoolmate in Glacier Creek, Jacqui Edwards, had known people here in Marietta. Jacqui's deceased husband had stayed with the Tierneys years ago. The families had stayed in touch and now the Teirney's daughter, Piper

Bloom, and Jacqui were friends.

Piper had lived in this small, furnished suite above her parents' garage until her marriage last year. The Tierneys weren't actively looking for a renter, which was why the space was available, but they explained that they used to put up young travelers all the time. They were happy to let her use it.

They were very hospitable, calling up this morning to offer breakfast and coffee since she didn't have her own groceries yet. She had joined them in their comfortable kitchen, meeting their ridiculously cheerful dog, Charlie. Then they had helped her to finish unpacking her car.

As Nicki told them about her new job, Mr. Tierney said he had probably played against Maury back when they were both on their respective high school basketball teams. The Tierneys had grown up in Livingston. The rivalry between the towns was fierce.

"I'll invite him for coffee," Mrs. Tierney said. "To bury the hatchet."

"Maury would love that," Nicki assured them, privately thinking, *Quincy will decline.*

Maury had unpacked his own room last night, calling across to Nicki at different times to ask for her help with holding open a garment bag and stacking a shoe box on a closet shelf. He was plainly excited by this fresh start in his old hometown, and even more eager to see his son and grandson settled here. Unfortunately, he was not physically capable of keeping up with his own ambitions. She had promised to finish his unpacking today, so he could take a bath last night and settle in for a well-deserved rest.

She was getting into her car, cringing from another biting wind under dull, flat clouds, when Mrs. Tierney came out of the front door and waved her down.

"Do they have a mixer and bowls? What about baking sheets?"

"Oh, you're a lifesaver! I didn't even think of that."

"Come. Borrow mine."

Minutes later, Nicki had a box of baking implements in the back of her car and slammed the hatch. She was ridiculously excited. She hadn't celebrated Christmas properly in years. Years and years, if she was honest. After her mother passed and her father remarried, her father and Gloria had put up a tree and hosted family dinners, but Gloria had her own way of doing things. She didn't have kids, but she was fond of her sister's children. They had been about Nicki's age and joined them for most holidays. It hadn't been awful, but it hadn't been the same as before.

Then, alone in California, Nicki had often wound up at misfit dinners where a handful of broke actors came together over potluck. It usually started out enjoyable enough, but it invariably turned into such hard partying she had been put off and left early. Worse, it occasionally became a passive-aggressive competition over who got what audition or part. Nicki had always left feeling battered and glum after those.

Now, for the first time in nearly fifteen years, she was anticipating the magic of Christmas. She was thinking about cookies, decorating, and *music*. "Jingle Bells" played in the empty grocery store as it opened. She hummed along as she picked up the handful of ingredients she needed for the shortbread recipe she'd looked up last night. As she headed to the cash register, she saw an Advent calendar and impulsively picked it up.

She hesitated, growing misty as she recalled the homemade one her mother had filled for her. She'd been so young when it started, she couldn't remember not having it. Each carefully sewn fabric pocket had been numbered and matched to a space on a big, felt tree. The gifts inside hadn't been extravagant, just a beaded bracelet or a pencil eraser shaped like an animal, maybe a wrapped candy or a rolled note that said, "I'm so proud of you!"

That first Christmas after her mother died, Nicki hung the calendar in her room like always, but Santa's elves hadn't filled it. When the second year rolled around, she left it in the box of her mother's keepsake ornaments and let Gloria hang the decorations she preferred.

Nicki swallowed and returned the mass-produced calendar onto its shelf. She had a better idea.

Actually, she was going to have to come up with twenty-five better ideas.

At least she had today's. *Make a homemade Advent calendar.*

QUINCY'S FIRST ORDER of business once he had his desk and computer properly set up was to figure out which side of the house he would extend to add an office.

It was far too distracting to be this close to the kitchen, especially with Nicki Darren in the house.

Was the music really necessary?

With a short-tempered sigh, he opened his browser and ordered a pair of noise-cancelling headphones. He'd been meaning to buy some anyway, since he would be traveling more.

He hated talking to strangers on a plane and didn't particularly like flying, but he was now working remotely, on contract, for his previous employer. Some people would appreciate the freedom in that arrangement. Others would take it as a good sign that the president had been willing to make accommodations to keep Quincy working for their firm in any way he could get him.

Quincy wasn't comforted. He liked predictability. Change irritated the hell out of him. Of course, changing up the Christmas carol would be nice. "Rudolf" *again*? *Really*?

Throwing himself to his feet, he pushed into the kitchen.

Today, Nicki wore a neon green T-shirt over a bright yellow long-sleeved body hugger. Her black pants were the clingy yoga kind. She had her head bent over her phone, loose hair falling in mahogany waves against her cheeks.

His father was nowhere to be found. Atlas stood on a

chair at the kitchen counter, squishing cookie dough through his fingers.

"Are you paying attention to what's happening over here?" Quincy moved behind Atlas to where the paper towels rolled off a holder beneath the cupboard. He pulled off a few sheets.

"Hmm?" Nicki stepped closer and peered into the bowl. "Oh, yes. Atlas is doing a great job. Are you tired of mixing?"

Atlas shook his head and dug into the dough with more intensity.

"We have a wooden spoon," Quincy pointed out. "He shouldn't be mixing with his hands."

"Purist, are you?" Her tone held a light tease. She snapped off her phone, conceding, "You're right. Most would say you shouldn't handle the butter when making shortbread, but this is a special recipe for kids, so it's okay. They also say you should make it in October, so it has time to cure. We're breaking all the rules with this batch. We're sugarplum rebels, aren't we, Atlas? Do you have a bill?"

Her quick switch of topic threw Quincy off the food-safety lecture he was about to deliver. "A bill? For what?"

"Anything. Any sort of mail that proves you live here."

"Why?"

"You need to show proof of residence to get a library card." She wiggled her phone. "That's what I was looking up."

"I don't need a library card. I have the Internet." Which

she knew, because she'd asked for his Wi-Fi code yesterday and had just looked something up.

"Atlas doesn't."

Quincy's first thought was that he could solve any lack of children's books with a one-click transaction, but he'd heard enough news reports cautioning against kids having too much screen time to figure out just as quickly that books on a *tablet* might not be the best move.

"Can't we order some to be delivered? How many does he need?"

"Kids are voracious. Frankly, I think you'll appreciate the variety even more than he will."

Quincy almost protested that he wasn't planning to read them, but the penny dropped. He *should* be reading with Atlas. That's what parents did. His parents had read to him.

He couldn't remember when he'd last read a book aloud. Back in grade school, he supposed. He'd blocked those memories because speaking in front of the class had paralyzed him. The recollection made him balk at the idea of reading aloud to Atlas.

His father came in from the garage.

"What about this one, Nicki?" Pops had a big sheet of cardboard from the packaging on Quincy's desk.

"Perfect! That'll make a nice big tree and we'll paint it green. Oh. Paint." She picked up the pad of multicolored sticky notes and wrote on it.

Quincy noticed several squares had been stuck to the

wall behind the kitchen table. Most held only a few words in her impulsive scrawl. One said, *Get a tree*. Another read, *Bake cookies*.

"The library has a special story time for kids tomorrow. We can bring Atlas to listen to that while we get him a card," Nicki told Pops. "Then he can pick out some books and we'll call that, 'Visit library for Christmas Books'." She scribbled a few words and stuck a fresh square to the wall. "We're making an Advent calendar," she told Quincy.

She might as well have spoken Swahili since he didn't see how notes about libraries stuck to the wall translated to— "One of those chocolate things with the little flaps that you get this time of year?"

"Kind of. Except ours is going to be fun activities to get ready for Christmas. We have, 'Get a tree,' of course." She used the clicker on the pen to point at the notes. "'Write a letter to Santa'. We should do that soon. 'Make sock puppets'? I'm still deciding if that's a good one. And 'Drive to see lights'. We'll give people a little more time to set up their displays before we do that one. Maury said there used to be something called a Christmas Stroll in Marietta. I'm wondering if there's a Santa Claus Parade or somewhere we can visit him. We'll ask at the library. They're sure to know all the community events. We'll have this filled in no time."

She kept saying, 'we' and 'us'.

"You're taking Pops and Atlas into town?" He glanced through the window where it was another bleak, icy day.

"I admit I felt rusty yesterday, driving the mountain passes, but I have really good tires. It's all coming back to me. Also, it's supposed to be sunny tomorrow. It will be okay."

Quincy should have been relieved. He really needed to get some work done. The promise of a quiet house was a blessing, but he was oddly uncomfortable with his father and Atlas being out of his sight.

"I made a list of a few things." He glanced around until he found the piece of paper with slippers and a robe on it. It had already occurred to him that he couldn't pick out clothing for Atlas without taking him. He wouldn't know the right size or color.

Strangely, he didn't want to entrust the task to his father or Nicki. He wanted to see what the stores had to offer and ensure Atlas was given the best they had. Maybe he didn't know how to be a parent, but after feeling judged so harshly by Karen's parents, he was determined to be a good provider, even if he was the only one to know it.

"I could come with you. To get these for him," he said.

"Oh. Ha! I thought that was your Christmas shopping list. I always got new pajamas when I was a kid. It was the gift we were allowed to open on Christmas Eve. Was that not a thing in your house?"

Quincy was insulted. He wouldn't give his kid *clothes* for Christmas. He'd already started looking up train sets and Lego kits.

But he was suddenly accosted by a memory of his mother

searching out a particular present, year after year, always taking her time selecting that special Christmas Eve gift. And yes, it had always turned out to be pajamas.

He scratched his hair, thinking back to the slight letdown of the gift being practical, not flashy or fun, but there had been something special about sleeping in those new pajamas. It meant the rest of the presents were only one more sleep away.

Now Quincy wondered if he should wait a couple of weeks to give Atlas his new pajamas and carry on that tradition. No, Atlas definitely needed new pajamas, but at least once Quincy knew the sizes, he could get another pair for Christmas Eve.

"He needs a robe and slippers regardless. It can't wait when it's this cold. I'll come with you," he decided.

"Okay." She looked wary.

He hadn't spoken too gruffly, had he? Some people found him dry and humorless, especially when he'd decided on a course of action and was ready to pursue it. He tried to find his most temperate tone.

"I have to get back to work. Is there a reason 'Rudolf' is on repeat?"

"Atlas is learning the words."

He glanced at the boy, who only blinked at him. The kid barely spoke. He wasn't going to sing.

Quincy sighed and turned away.

"A bill for the Internet would probably do it," Nicki said behind him. "For the library card."

December 2nd

THE NEXT MORNING, Nicki was putting away the dishes from the dishwasher while Atlas ate his cereal when Maury came in, hair akimbo and face unshaven.

Since he had to check his glucose level before he ate, she took the opportunity to sit down with her notebook and learn more about his health, taking his blood pressure and reviewing his records herself.

He seemed very diligent, keeping a logbook of what he ate and when he took his meds, along with his readings. Until a few weeks ago, he'd been fairly stable.

"Your blood pressure has been spiking," she observed. "It's a little high today." She recorded it for him.

"My sugar levels are off, too." Maury looked tired. "It's been a busy few weeks with the move and everything."

He glanced at Atlas, who was watching intently as she gathered the blood pressure cuff to put it away.

"Do you want to feel it?" she asked the boy. "It's like a big hug. I can do it on your leg."

He shook his head and went back to chasing the last bran

flakes in his bowl.

"If you change your mind, just tell me. Your Pops and I are going to do this pretty often for the next little while." Glancing over Maury's logbook again, she asked, "I don't suppose you've had time to find a doctor here yet?"

"It's not that bad, is it?" He brought the book back under his own nose and put on his glasses.

"No, but I'm thinking sooner than later is better. And maybe you should have a down day." She patted his shoulder, feeling him sigh.

Maury nodded. "I was thinking the same thing. Until you showed up yesterday, I haven't felt like I could." He frowned, sidling a glance at Atlas, who was holding his bowl like a cup, draining the milk.

"All done?" Nicki asked the boy. "Did you have enough? Do you want more?"

Atlas shook his head.

"How about you get dressed, then? Call me if you need me. I'm going to make Pops some breakfast."

Atlas climbed off his chair. He carried his bowl and spoon to the counter, then came back to push in his chair before leaving the kitchen.

"He's a really sweet boy," Nicki said, watching him go.

"Too quiet, though. I haven't heard him laugh. Doesn't even smile."

"He's sad. It's understandable. *Your* blood pressure is up from this move, and it was your choice. He's adjusting to a lot. Scrambled eggs okay?"

"I can make my own eggs."

"But you don't *have* to. This is what I'm getting paid for. Take it easy and let me do it. Tell me why you were so determined to move back to your old home." She set out the non-stick pan, then went to the refrigerator for eggs. "You said you were planning to move back here alone. That's a big decision if your son was in Philadelphia."

"I asked him to come with me. More than once. He's stubborn. And he had a very good job." Maury rubbed his thumb and fingers together, indicating that Quincy's job paid well. "I didn't blame him for wanting to stick with it, but…" He shook his head. "The city was never the right place for him. My wife had family there, and she wasn't one for change either. I tried so many times to talk her into moving here, but she wouldn't. I always wanted to come back though. When this house came up and it was only me, I thought, well, I'll move and my son will have to visit me. Maybe that will convince him."

"Sneaky." She wrinkled her nose and smiled as she whipped the eggs. "Then Atlas came to live with him full time, so he decided they would join you?"

Maury closed his logbook and slid it aside. "Quincy didn't know about Atlas until a few weeks ago."

"Oh." Her gaze flicked to the door into the dining room. She suddenly felt like they were gossiping. She had speculated, of course, but now she took in what a shock that must have been for all of them. "No wonder he seems…" She searched for a nice way to say it. "Out of his depth."

Yesterday, after the cookies were done, she had set two on a plate and held Atlas's hand as they delivered them to his father.

Quincy had stared at the plate for several ticks of the nearby clock before taking in her expression, then Atlas's. She had seen his reluctance. The boy's hands had been in the dough, but he wasn't obtuse. He wasn't *mean*. After a moment, he'd said, "Thank you," then picked up a cookie to take a bite.

Say, 'Mmm good,' she wanted to chide. *Pick up the boy, hug him. Tell him you can taste the love. Say it's the best cookie you've ever had in your life.*

Instead, she'd been the one to crouch next to Atlas, to hug and praise him. Then they'd gone back to the kitchen to put away the rest of the cooled cookies.

Maury held a pained frown. "Atlas is so like him. Quincy doesn't see it, but I do. It makes me feel as though I have a second chance. I traveled for work when Quincy was young. I missed so much. I let him down."

"You're being hard on yourself. Parents work. That's reality. And grandparents are supposed to be the ones who have time for their grandkids. It's good he decided to join you. Really good for Atlas."

Maury snorted. "He tried to talk me into staying there with him. I showed him stubborn." His sidelong look brimmed with self-satisfaction.

She shot him a grin, but he wasn't looking at her. He was sobering into a frown of introspection.

"This is a second chance for all of us," Maury said, as though reassuring himself. "I can be a better father to my own son, and maybe he'll…" He didn't finish.

Her heart caught at the dejection she read in him.

"He will," Nicki assured him, thinking of the way Quincy had eaten both of the cookies despite his reservations. "He just needs time."

And opportunity.

She lifted her gaze off the eggs she was pushing around the pan and glanced at the notes for the Advent calendar still stuck to the wall.

Hmm.

QUINCY STARTED UP the stairs and caught Atlas as he was coming down.

The boy was singing, "*Woo-doff wiff yoh nose so bwight, won' chew gwide my sway to—*"

Atlas froze when he saw Quincy and bit his lips together.

Quincy's first impulse was to correct him. *Ru*dolf.

He flashed back to the years it had taken him to master that sound. He replayed Atlas's rendition, heard all the soft Rs.

Damn. Would he need speech therapy, too?

On the heels of that came the voices of his grade-school tormentors, mocking, "*Thah-WA-pee.*"

Quincy bit his own lips together, not wanting to speak ever again in this lifetime.

His chest felt tight, while something ferocious roared awake in his blood. Something with claws and teeth that wanted to tear apart those who might even think of teasing Atlas, driving back anyone who might negatively impact the boy's budding confidence.

Atlas stood with his enormous brown eyes fixed on Quincy's face.

Quincy pulled himself together, pushing the anger back into its bottle and doing his best to find a calm, non-threatening expression.

"We, uh…" Quincy had to clear his throat. "We can listen to that song in the car if you want. When we go to the library."

THE INTERIOR OF the Marietta library was decorated with colorful, blinking lights, cutout snowflakes, and red-and-green paper chains. One wall was covered in entries from the Draw Santa contest. The central table held a display of books about Christmas, Hanukkah, and Kwanzaa.

Nicki took Atlas across to the small group of children gathered around the storyteller, a woman of retired age who introduced herself as Louise. She was reading *The Grinch*

Who Stole Christmas and warmly invited Atlas to join them.

Nicki then searched out a scrap of paper and a pencil from the lending counter to make notes for her Advent calendar. Along with the homemade decorations they could replicate, she noticed the tree was decorated with little cards in the shape of angels. Each one was labeled with the age and sex of a child in need.

Donate a gift. *Brilliant.*

There was a notice that the regular Family Game Night at the library was on hiatus until January. Those sorts of board games were probably too advanced for Atlas, but she would look in the thrift store for something age appropriate. The workshop for making a pinecone bird feeder had potential, too.

A poster hung on the door, advertising the Christmas Stroll. It included a Gingerbread House competition, but they'd missed the deadline to enter, *darn it*. They could still make one, she decided, writing it down with everything else. The Stroll was this weekend. When she read the list of events, she did a mental fist pump. *Yes, yes, yes!* Such a great activity for her calendar.

And Quincy.

He was such a baffling man! He'd worn an expression close to grim as they had piled into the car, but he was the one who had put on the Christmas carols so Atlas could listen to "Rudolf".

Now he wore a stern profile as he finished up the process

of getting his lending card along with a child's card for Atlas.

The older woman behind the counter smiled with dazzled attraction as she explained the fine points of reserving books online.

Nicki couldn't blame her. Quincy was the definition of the strong, silent type, not even nodding in understanding as the woman stammered through her spiel. At the same time, he stood tall and commanding. His puffy winter jacket managed to showcase his broad shoulders and long legs. He had enough of a rugged look to seem like he belonged in Montana, but he was missing the cowboy boots and hat that were as common here as they were in Texas.

He dazzled *her* without even glancing in her direction.

Tingling, Nicki joined him and smiled as the woman finished up. "Do you happen to know where we can get a tree?"

"Oh, I'm sorry." The woman grew even more flustered. "I didn't realize your wife was with you. We should make her a card, too."

"I'm not—"

"She's actually my—" Quincy cut himself off, regarding Nicki with a perplexed kink in his dark brow.

Nicki could practically hear him running through the labels. *Father's nurse? Son's nanny? Housekeeper?*

"Christmas elf?" she suggested.

"Employee."

The flat way he said it swept all the air out of her sails.

Nicki reminded herself she was a big girl who wasn't living on approval any longer. She *was* his employee. Lucky her, that meant she still got a paycheck even if he didn't like the way she played her role.

It still felt like a rebuff.

The librarian wasn't sure what to make of them, Nicki could tell.

"I use a fake one," the woman stammered. "But there's a tree farm outside of town. I'll look up the directions."

"Excuse me," a woman said from behind them. Nicki turned to see the newcomer. She was blonde and pretty, looked to be in her late thirties, and carried a toddler on her hip.

The little girl pointed at the children in the corner, and the woman said, "Oh, sure, honey. Go sit with the kids." She lowered the toddler to the floor. "Here. Let me take your coat, first. Sorry," she said as she straightened, tugging the sleeves of her daughter's jacket. "I couldn't help overhearing that you're looking for a tree. My stepson works at Scott's. It's easy to find. In fact, I have the flyer."

She tucked her daughter's coat under her arm and dug into her shoulder bag.

"This is from when they were advertising for students to apply. Let me just get my grocery list." She tore off a corner. "You still have the address." She handed it to Nicki with a smile. "It's a nice outing for kids. Horse-drawn sleigh, cocoa, and cookies. Music."

"Are you in marketing?" Nicki teased. "Because that's an excellent sales pitch."

The blonde laughed. "No commission, just being neighborly. Are you new here?"

"We are. I'm Nicki Darren. This is Quincy Ryan and that's his son, Atlas, in blue. His father was born here, though. Did you know the Ryans at all?"

"No, I'm from California. I still feel new to town myself, but everyone is always so friendly. I'm Liz Canon."

"Oh, where in California? I was living…"

THE WOMEN CONNECTED like a pair of magnets, sidelining Quincy—which didn't bother him. It was very much his comfort zone. He didn't want to talk or be talked to. At least Nicki wasn't flitting all over the library anymore, like a budgie loose from its cage.

That allowed him to keep all his attention on Atlas. This was Quincy's first time in public with the boy, without his father for additional support. It felt like a lot of responsibility. What if Atlas decided to throw a tantrum the way some kids did? What if he wandered off?

Judging by the lack of hovering parents in the story zone, people didn't steal children here, but Quincy still wore a cloak of city caution.

Plus, ever since he heard Atlas singing this morning, he'd been worrying about the boy going to school and being around other children. Kids could be heartless about the smallest things.

Was Atlas having trouble with his speech? He wanted to ask the boy about it, but knew from experience that being forced to talk might be the kid's worst nightmare. He could call Karen's parents later—Except, *damn*. They'd gone to Australia for the holidays, to see their son. That was another reason they hadn't wanted custody of Atlas. They had plans that didn't include a child they only saw intermittently. Email, then, he decided.

"Oh, sorry about that," Liz said as her daughter joined the group of seated children, toddling between them to set a familiar hand on Atlas's shoulder and plunk herself beside him. "Lucy is still learning the 'hands to yourself' rule."

Atlas didn't seem to mind, only looked at her, then wiggled over to make room.

"Such a gentleman," Nicki said with a warmth and affection that wormed into Quincy's heart. He liked that she liked his son. He didn't know why that pleased him so much. He couldn't take any credit for how Atlas conducted himself, but it still gave Quincy a little kick of pride each time she showed approval toward the boy.

As Lucy sat down next to Atlas, legs stuck out straight before her, she turned her head and beamed at Atlas. It was a silent, *Isn't this great?*

Atlas gazed at her for a long time. Slowly, a real smile, the first Quincy had seen, dawned on the little boy's face. It wasn't one of those friendly grins that Nicki and Pops knew how to throw around, either. It was heartfelt, welcoming, and sweet. The little boy's heart opened up right there, innocently and completely, under the sunny expression of the little girl who had touched his shoulder.

"Oh..." Nicki sighed. "That is the cutest thing I've seen in my life."

"I think we just witnessed an actual bloom of love." Liz sounded almost reverent.

Quincy knotted up on Atlas's behalf. Didn't he know you had to keep your cards close to your chest?

Quincy wanted to stop what was happening before his eyes, to warn his son not to let any feeling ever be so strong, not to let his emotions show so nakedly. The kid might as well have been teetering off the edge of a building, given how suffocated Quincy felt by the impending danger of the boy's unfettered reaction. He was helpless to save him.

"It's nice to see him smile like that, isn't it?" Nicki directed her question up to Quincy.

Quincy felt sick.

Atlas turned his attention back to Louise, but he wiggled his bum closer to Lucy.

"How long will story time take?" Quincy asked, hearing the abruptness in his tone, but unable to temper it. "I need to pick up an extension cord at the hardware store."

"We'll be here long enough for you to do that." Nicki's tone grew a shade cooler. "Atlas will need to choose some books to bring home after. And your dad wanted us to grab some Christmas lights while we're out," she reminded as he started to walk away. "You could probably find some there."

The season of joy. *Right.*

December 3rd

AS IF THE house wasn't already more colorful than a Persian market, Quincy was enlisted to hang lights all day Saturday while his father set up one of those gaudy, life-sized Santa and reindeer cutouts on the front yard.

Nicki had had the foresight to suggest a snowsuit for Atlas while they were out yesterday, so she and Atlas joined him outside, making snow angels and building a snowman between holding the ladder and 'providing artistic guidance'. She had also asked him to help her lift the body of the snowman onto its base, but let Atlas arrange the rocks on his face around the carrot nose before she put the head on herself.

"And look what I have for a hat!" She set a red sand pail upside down on the frozen man's head. "He's handsome, isn't he?"

His cockeyed expression made him look drunk, but Quincy kept his mouth shut.

When they went inside, Nicki made cocoa with mini-marshmallows and whipped up a fresh batch of cookie dough that had to refrigerate overnight. "Best Ever Sugar Cookies," she promised. "When they're cool, we'll decorate them."

Quincy made do with the shortbread, which was really good, and took some to his desk with his cocoa.

Nicki followed him. "I'm going to let Atlas watch a movie this afternoon, so he's not too tired when we go out to the Stroll tonight."

"I thought you said it was a couple of blocks in town. We look at the lights on a few houses until he gets tired, then come home. Right?"

"Oh, um." She chuckled. "That's not what I meant when I said 'Christmas Stroll'. It's a thing. An event." She explained that the main street would be blocked off to traffic and local businesses were scheduled to stay open late, so people could shop and mingle, enjoying street entertainment and food tents.

His brain blanked. That was the sort of thing other people did. His father loved parades and company picnics, but not Quincy. Once he reached adulthood, he had made the choice to avoid crowds. Watching fireworks was great, but from the balcony of his apartment. He didn't want to walk down to the beach on the Fourth of July and rub shoulders with a bunch of strangers.

She chewed the corner of her mouth, finally breaking the silence to say, "I think he would like it. There will be carolers and hay rides."

Was that a warning? Because it didn't sound like an incentive.

"You could probably get him a stocking. Maybe he could even visit Santa."

Quincy knew he was behaving like the green creature with the small heart, but he'd never enjoyed having anything crammed down his throat. Besides, this didn't sound like *Christmas*. It sounded like he'd be drinking uncut commercialism, straight from the bottle.

Pops came in at that point and said he wanted to go. He hadn't had a proper chance to walk downtown and mingle with the locals yet, reacquainting with the changes since he'd lived here as a child. Nicki ran out a little while later to pick up the buttons that acted as a pass for the event, but Pops paid for them.

So Quincy swallowed his dissention, bundled up as it grew dark, and drove the bunch of them to the library where they parked the SUV. He still missed his Corolla. A pickup truck seemed the vehicle of choice in Marietta, but midrange SUVs were also popular. Given he was working from home and no longer commuting, the lower mileage wasn't an issue and even though he hadn't had to use the four-wheel drive yet, he was glad he had it.

He would have happily driven them wherever they wanted to go, but they walked across to Crawford Park and caught a hayride. *Him*. A city boy who hadn't seen a real, live cow until he took a bus upstate for math camp in Grade

Ten.

As they reached the rodeo fair grounds, Pops said to Atlas, "We'll come out here next year when the rodeo is on."

Quincy just wanted to get through Christmas.

He sat as still on the hay bale as Atlas did, while Pops and Nicki chattered with the other families aboard the wagon, sharing where they were from, how long it had been since they'd done this, and how much fun they'd always had.

It wasn't bad. The ambling wagon allowed them to see that people were coming from all directions, families carrying little ones and pushing strollers, older couples and teens circulating. It was rare to see an event draw all ages like this. There was no sense of urgency, either, which Quincy had to admit was refreshing. No city tension where hustle and bustle and staking of territory was the name of the game. Everyone moved like they had no particular place to be. They were just… strolling.

The wagon let them off, and they made their way to Main Street where the scent of frying foods and hot cider floated on the air. Colored lights were suspended across the road, glowing green, yellow, red, and blue against the night sky. The spill of light from the shops reflected off the tiny snowflakes drifting in the air. All the windows wore bright displays framed with garlands and reflective snowflakes and blinking mini lights. A choir sang "Silver Bells," almost drowned out by the laughter and conversation of the milling crowd.

"Well, isn't this a picture," Pops said, breath clouding. He hung back to take in the vision.

Quincy had to admit it was different from what he'd imagined. *Festive.*

"Ho' my han'," Atlas said, wiggling his mitted fingers into Quincy's gloved palm. "So I don' get yost."

Lost, Quincy almost corrected, but offered two curled fingers for Atlas to grip, then secured the boy's hold with the light press of his thumb.

Curiosity pulled him forward, drawing Atlas with him. Atlas held out his other hand for Nicki to take. They wound their way into the melee, pausing when they came upon the carolers who switched up to "Hark! The Herald Angels Sing".

Atlas couldn't take his eyes off the woman in the elf hat with its big, pointed ears. She smiled and waved at them.

"We want to make our way to the Graff Hotel," Nicki said. "Photo with Santa. It also has the gingerbread house competition. We want to get some ideas for our own. Don't we, Atlas?"

Atlas nodded, so they headed there first. As they walked, Pops provided a commentary. "My uncle had a lawnmower repair shop at the end of that street. I broke my arm, falling off my bicycle right on that corner when I was nine. I was delivering papers and my tire blew. Did you know Chase Goodwin is from Marietta? The ball player. Back in my day, we all tried out for baseball, but you had to get your name on the list, here in this building, when it was the Sport and Hunt. That's how they got you to come in and buy a glove."

The hotel was packed with people shuffling past the gingerbread houses, but it was worth the close quarters. The houses were incredibly intricate and deserved a thorough study. The whole place smelled like Christmas—cinnamon, ginger, nutmeg, and molasses.

"This might be above our level, Atlas," Nicki said, brow furrowing as she took in a gingerbread church with a stained glass window made from cooled liquid sugar and food coloring.

Quincy found his gaze lingering on her expression more than the houses. She was entranced, dark eyes reflecting little glints as she took in scrolls and scallops of icing, gumdrop stepping stones and candy-canes archways.

"Oh, look! It's a whole village. It's Marietta! Look, Maury!" She was so excited Quincy felt his mouth twitch with amusement.

It's candy, he wanted to point out, but a woman invited Atlas to climb a short stepladder, so he could better see a gingerbread carousel with plastic horses.

Atlas kept Quincy's fingers in his fist as he climbed, then looked at the carousel that plinked with calliope music as it slowly turned.

"How can it move?" Atlas asked the woman. "It's food."

"I don't know," she admitted. "I didn't make it."

Atlas frowned with puzzlement.

Quincy pointed under the rotating disk that made the

floor of the carousel. "There's a tiny motor under there."

The boy crouched and squinted.

Quincy's mouth twitched again. He'd been exactly that inquisitive as a kid, wanting to know how stuff worked. It was how he'd wound up drawing electrical schematics for a living.

"You probably can't see it. I'll find a picture on my computer and show you tomorrow."

" 'kay." Atlas came down off the step, still holding tightly to Quincy's fingers.

That was when Quincy realized Nicki had joined them. She wore the look women got when they saw a newborn, as if he and Atlas were too cute for words.

Scowling with self-consciousness, Quincy said, "Should we go see Santa?"

They made their way to the line where people waited with their children. The gathered crowd made, "Ah," noises as each child took his or her spot on Santa's lap.

Atlas held back when his turn came up.

Quincy didn't need Nicki's hurried, "It's okay," to keep him from pressing Atlas into being the center of attention. He wouldn't force him to do something like that if he didn't want to.

"Probably wise," Pops said as they left the hotel. "When your mother took you for photos with Santa, every shot showed the back of your throat."

Nicki looked at Quincy, pursed her mouth for one second, then burst out laughing.

December 4th

"I CAN TAKE him myself if you don't want to come," Nicki said the next morning. "Liz said there will be boys there to help tie the tree to the car."

"No, I'll come." Quincy hadn't looked happy about it, though, and had been at his computer right up until she was helping Atlas into his new boots and mittens.

Maury bowed out again.

The quiet morning the other day had done Maury a world of good. He'd been rejuvenated when they arrived home from the library, eager to read aloud the books Atlas had selected. Yesterday had been another busy day, however, with being outside in the yard, then walking around town. Maury was better off resting, and he wanted to start making calls to old friends here in Marietta, to reconnect.

Which meant she was on her own with Quincy again.

She thought they had made progress last night. He had laughed with her over the remark his father had made about his reaction to visiting Santa. Shortly after, they'd moved along the Stroll to enter a shop showcasing local crafters.

After much deliberation over colors and styles, the Ryans all had their names embroidered onto Christmas stockings.

Watching them had made Nicki quite wistful. They had already arranged for Christmas Eve to be her last day of work. She was driving to Glacier Creek that night to spend Christmas with her father and Gloria—her first in years.

It was important she do that. Seeing the disjointed relationship between Quincy and his son made her realize how much she had let her relationship with her own father deteriorate. It was time to move past old hurts, no matter how difficult that might be.

She put that out of her mind, concentrating instead on the winter wonderland around them. The sky was so blue, the snow so pristine, she didn't want anything to ruin her enjoyment of the day.

"I missed this so much," Nicki said as she gazed across the peaceful landscape. "I used to tell people how glad I was to be away from the cold and shoveling, but there's something about having well-defined seasons that feels right. Like you're part of nature's process."

Silence.

She looked at Quincy's noncommittal profile, then at Atlas in the backseat. He was buckled into his booster, also staring out at the empty, snow-blanketed fields. There was quiet curiosity in his expression. She hoped it was a sign that Montana was working on him. Healing was hard in traffic and crowds, surrounded by concrete.

Here, among nature and mountains, you could find yourself again.

She hoped to rediscover her own self, anyway.

And the Ryan men seemed to like the quiet, she thought with private amusement. Hopefully, Atlas would grow up seeing Montana as home. Not just the place he lived, but home, in his heart.

"Maybe that's why your father wanted to move back here," she mused.

"We had seasons in Philly."

"Oh. I meant… It doesn't matter. Do you miss it, though?" she asked, curious now that Quincy seemed willing to talk. "Are you homesick for Philadelphia?"

"Nothing feels familiar, so yeah. There was a really nice bakery on my block, and it was easier to work in my office where I could shut the door."

That was it? He was homesick for a loaf of bread and the isolation of his office?

"What kind of work do you do, exactly? I saw your business card said draftsman. Do you design houses?"

"I work for an architectural firm. We mostly design commercial buildings. I specialize in electrical drawings, but I can do structural ones if needed."

"You draw on the computer?"

"With a program, yes." He said it like he'd had to explain it many times.

"You should show Atlas."

Quincy glanced at her, frowning. "Why?"

"Because he would probably like to know what you're doing, since you're on your computer all the time. Would you like to see, Atlas?" She glanced back at him.

Atlas nodded.

"It's pretty complex."

"Draw something simple. Oh, I know! Draw the tree for our Advent calendar."

Quincy's mouth opened and shut as if he wanted to protest. He wound up sending her a scowl that wasn't exactly disapproving, but a tiny bit dismayed. "That's definitely simple."

"Not for me." She shrugged. "I was going to draw one freehand, but I've been holding off, certain I'd ruin our one good piece of cardboard. Maury said his hands shake too much. You're our guy," she decided.

He didn't say anything because they arrived at the tree farm. He turned into the driveway and parked next to a handful of other vehicles, near some snow-swept picnic tables.

It was already shaping up to be a busy day with people milling in and out of the decorated tents, as well as trailing into the forest of pre-cut and newly potted trees. As they climbed from the SUV, the chill hit, but at least the wind had stopped. The air was filled with the damp scent of sawdust and evergreen boughs. Tinny loudspeakers played "Frosty the Snowman".

"That smells like Christmas, doesn't it?" She took Atlas's mitted hand in her gloved one. "Shall we get some hot chocolate so we can drink it while we choose a tree?"

The atmosphere was casual, yet operated like a well-oiled machine with a handful of teenagers mixed in with the adults as they sold cookies and dealt with all the people coming and going.

The sleigh would be back in a few minutes, they were told, and were invited to visit the tents if they wanted hot drinks, baking, or homemade wreaths.

Steam rose in little wisps from the spouts of all the thermoses at the drinks table. The girl behind it was quick to explain. "This one is homemade cocoa, this one's hot cider, and this one is Irish Cream hot chocolate, but it's only flavored that way. No alcohol."

"Have you tried hot cider before, Atlas? You can try mine. If you don't like it, you can have the cocoa." Nicki asked the girl to pour a tiny sip and swirled it a moment. The aroma of cinnamon and cloves made her sigh with nostalgia, and the sub-zero air quickly cooled it to drinkable. She offered it to the boy.

He didn't care for it, but Nicki had the cup filled for herself and snapped a lid over it, then added extra milk to Atlas's cocoa before covering his.

Quincy didn't want a drink, but he paid even though she had her wallet out. Then he pushed a twenty into the tip jar.

"Thank you," Nicki said as they meandered away, adding, "That was really generous."

He gave her a little frown. "It's Christmas."

Nicki couldn't argue with that and only pointed out the gingerbread men at the cookie table.

"Look at these," she said to Atlas. "I want to make a house for one of these guys with you. I bet we could make a man like this to live in it. Not tomorrow, though. We have to take Pops to the doctor and make a pinecone bird feeder."

"We're leaving the house *again?*" Quincy said.

She couldn't help it. She released a peal of laughter. "It's five minutes into town. Is that so *bad?*"

He made a face, scowling at her when she continued to laugh.

"I'm sorry. I didn't realize how much you liked staying home. You're jealous of your father right now, aren't you?"

"Insanely."

"Well, I was hoping you'd take Atlas to the workshop, but you don't have to. It's just that it's at the same time as your father's appointment. I was going to go in with your father, to introduce myself to his new doctor. But I'm sure your father can handle his own appointment. I can take Atlas."

"No," Quincy grumbled. "Check in with his doctor. I'll do the pinecone thing. What about these?" He indicated the butter tarts.

"Are you asking if I want one? Or whether I can make them? I'm hopeless with pastry, so no. If you want one, you should get one here."

He asked for six and handed over another twenty, refusing the change.

The woman behind the counter winked at Atlas and offered him a gingerbread man free of charge.

Atlas hesitated, looking to Nicki. She looked to Quincy.

He shrugged his shoulders. "Sure?" he answered, but he didn't sound sure.

Oh, this man.

"You can have it," she told Atlas, "But remember your manners."

Atlas took it with a shy, "Tank you." Then he held it and stared at it.

"Should we ask your dad to put it in the bag with the butter tarts, so it doesn't get lost or broken?" Nicki suggested.

Atlas nodded, and Quincy took it, saying, "I'll put them in the Bronco."

Atlas sipped his cocoa as they approached the table of wreaths and other decorations. He lowered his cup to take a long look at the candy-cane reindeer with pipe-cleaner antlers, googly eyes, and tiny pompoms for noses.

"This one is supposed to be Rudolf. See his red nose?"

Atlas's brown eyes flicked up to hers. He gave her a tiny smile. "It's candy."

"It is. But you don't eat them right away. You hang them on the tree as a decoration. Should we buy a few?"

He nodded.

"Six please."

"For an extra dollar, you get the whole team," the young man behind the table said.

"Well, we'd better do that, then. We can't leave anyone behind, can we?" She set down her cider to get out her wallet while the young man behind the table encouraged Atlas to point to the ones he wanted, helping him name them as they went.

"I've got it," Quincy said behind her, handing over another of his crisp twenties.

She was so startled by his sudden appearance, her pulse leapt. At least, she told herself it was his surprise arrival, but her blood continued to simmer with awareness as he stayed next to her, scanning the table.

He had more than exceeded the price for the reindeer, but he said, "We'll take a wreath for the door, too," and offered another twenty.

She looked at his stern expression framed in that dark beard, seeing her sober, Grinchy boss with new eyes. He was an absolute soft touch under that façade. If he was this generous with business transactions, what would he be like at the drive for the food bank she had added to the calendar for next week?

"I'll stow this, too," Quincy said as the sleigh returned with a group of laughing families. "You go ahead to the sleigh. I don't need to ride it."

Like heck he didn't. "We'll ask them to wait."

She caught a flash of alarm in Atlas's eyes as Quincy turned away. She caught Quincy's arm to stop him.

He looked from her hand to her face, something flickering in his gaze. His arm felt really tense and muscled, even beneath the pockets of down filler.

"Do you want to hold one of the candy canes?" she asked Atlas, pretending it was totally normal to touch your boss, but letting go of him as she spoke.

Atlas nodded, but he sidled a cautious glance to Quincy. He wasn't afraid of his father, but she suspected he was equal parts intimidated by the big man with the big voice, while he yearned for Quincy's approval without even understanding that was what he was looking for.

"Oh. Okay. Be careful. It might break." Quincy flicked Nicki a glance that suggested he wasn't sure this was a good idea, but he offered Atlas one of the reindeer.

Atlas hesitated, gaze going to the ones Quincy still held.

"You want Rudolf?" she guessed. "The one with the red nose?"

Atlas nodded.

"Oh." Quincy frowned, obviously not having noticed there was a difference. He switched up the candies and took the rest to the SUV with the wreath.

"Who's next?" the sleigh driver called.

Nicki walked Atlas across to where the red sleigh was stationed behind two enormous draft horses. Their signature scent coated the air. One snorted, releasing a plume of mist above his nose.

Atlas's little hand tightened in hers.

"I'm sure it's very safe, but we'll wait for your dad—"

"Nicki!"

She turned to see Liz picking her way across the frozen parking lot toward them, Lucy on her hip.

"I was just dropping Ethan for work and saw Quincy, so I knew you were here." Liz pointed to where a young man was pulling on gloves and heading into the thick of the cut trees.

The young man lifted his arm in a friendly wave, calling, "Morning, Lane."

The sleigh driver called back, "Morning, Ethan." Then to Liz, "How are you, Liz? How's Blake?"

"We're all great, Lane. Thanks. You?"

Lane responded in kind, then turned to help a family settle into the sleigh.

"I'm dropping Lucy in town with my brother and heading to the airport to pick up my other daughter," Liz said. "The usual Christmas shuffle. But I wanted to say hi again and tell you... I mentioned to my sister-in-law that Lucy has a suitor. She said you're her parents' new tenant?"

"Oh, the Tierneys? Piper is your sister-in-law? What a coincidence!"

"Not in this town. Not really. Everyone knows everyone and winds up related by marriage if not by blood."

Nicki nodded, accepting that since Glacier Creek was much the same.

"But we're having a toboggan day soon, out at the ranch. Depends on the weather and Ethan's day off. I wanted to invite you to bring Atlas. It's a great day for the kids—No, sweetie, you can't go in the sleigh." She caught her daughter from trying to pitch out of her arms. "You're going to see Uncle Sea Bass. Oh. It's not the sleigh you want. Hi, Atlas." Liz smiled at him. "How are you today? Are you having fun?"

Atlas nodded, gaze fixed with adoration on Lucy.

Why wouldn't he be besotted? Lucy wore a purple hat with matching mittens. Her hat had teddy bear ears with pink centers. She grinned at Atlas and pointed at Pup-pup, the stuffed dog he liked to carry.

"Oh, that's his special toy, honey," Nicki told the girl.

Without an ounce of hesitation, Atlas held out his candy-cane Rudolf. "Be cah-fow. Dey bwake."

"Oh, sweetie, you don't have to give her that," Liz said. "That one is yours. We can buy one for her ourselves."

But Lucy wanted it, and Atlas wanted her to have it.

"This love affair is going to kill me with how cute it is," Liz said. "But I do have to run. Take my card, though, and pop me an email, so I have yours. I'll send you the date and directions."

"You have a spa?" Nicki asked, then recognized the logo and the name of the chain. "I've been to one of your salons in L.A!"

"My mom and sister run those. I run a retreat at the ranch in the summer. I'll show it to you when you come out."

Her gaze lifted and she smiled. Nicki's neck tingled. Quincy was back.

"We'll see you soon," Liz said, wrestling her increasingly wiggly daughter. "No, we have to go," she insisted, earning a cry of protest as she carried Lucy to the car.

Atlas watched her go with a forlorn look in his eyes.

"It's okay, honey. We'll see her again soon. Let's get in the sleigh. People are waiting." She scooted in and added, "Why don't you sit on your dad's knee so you can see better?"

She was being sneaky, forcing some contact between father and son, but it worked. Quincy wore a neutral expression as he settled Atlas on his lap. Lane handed them a red-and-green blanket, saying, "The breeze is chilly."

Seconds later, the horse took off at a trot. The bells started to jangle and cold air cut across her cheeks. The family with them began singing a rousing chorus of, "Dashing Through the Snow," which made her smile.

The air smelled fresh and the *whooshing* noise of the sleigh against the snow made it feel like they were flying. Atlas smiled as though he had a secret, which made Nicki grin even wider.

Quincy glanced at her and tucked his hand more securely

around his son, his face relaxing.

Which was when Nicki knew she was in trouble. Not the kind of trouble that came from crushing on her handsome boss, either.

His gaze swept with interest to the rugged mountains, rolling fields, and the line of trees as they trotted down the perimeter of the farm. She caught her breath, wanting him to like it here. Feel at home.

She wanted him to be happy.

She wanted to *make* him happy.

QUINCY HATED MEETING new people. Work mixers where he was supposed to make small talk with clients were his worst nightmare. One of the reasons he loved the city was its anonymity. It might be overrun with people, but it wasn't necessary to talk to them beyond, "Excuse me," and "Good morning."

Sharing a sleigh with strangers made him stifle a sigh, especially when they started singing and Nicki joined in.

Atlas might have felt the same. When Nicki suggested he sing too, Atlas only shrank into Quincy like he was seeking protection.

The action caused a strange feeling to coil around Quincy's heart. The constriction didn't hurt. It felt weirdly good. Like a hug. Holding his son was like cradling the warm body of an oversized puppy. He felt protective, scared of hurting him, and privileged all at once. But holding a child, *his* child, was bizarrely profound. He could barely take it in.

When the sleigh came back to its starting point and halted, he realized he'd only been thinking about Atlas and his comfort. He'd stopped thinking about the work waiting for him at home or whether he was happy to be here or not.

It was disturbing. What was next? Falling on his back and making snow angels?

He waited for the other family to disembark, then set Atlas on his feet outside the sleigh. "Let's get this tree picked."

The boy didn't move, only stared across to where the mini forest of trees was being invaded by a group of school-aged students. A field trip of some kind?

Before he thought it through, Quincy heard himself say, "Do you want me to carry you?"

He didn't know why he said it. It was the lingering thoughts of puppies, protection, and places to get lost. The bigger children looked overexcited and liable to knock over a little boy without even seeing him, like bulls in a china shop.

Atlas turned and nodded, holding up his arms.

Quincy reached down, but then he wasn't sure how to carry him. Lucy had clung to her mother's hip like a monkey, but that seemed kind of girly. For both him and Atlas.

"Shoulders?" he suggested, and hoisted Atlas up.

Little hands clutched the top of his fisherman's cap. Atlas

made a noise that sounded—

Quincy shot a look at Nicki. "Did he just—?" *Chuckle?*

She nodded, a bright look in her eye as she took out her phone and snapped a photo.

The binding around Quincy's heart gave another squeeze, like something was being anchored to it, the ties tightening. He swallowed and closed his hands firmly around his son's skinny, denim-clad calves. Atlas's boots dug into his chest.

"You like it up there, don't you, Atlas?" Nicki said with a lilt of emotion in her voice. "It's a good spot for seeing all the best trees." Were her lips trembling? "That was a really good idea, Quincy." She squeezed his arm.

It wasn't throwaway praise. It was sincere. And even though he barely knew her and would swear on a stack of bibles that he didn't care what she thought of him, it meant something to him that she smiled up at him as though he possessed heroic qualities.

He was actively trying not to like her. He'd been trying to freeze her out all morning. She was too chipper, too outgoing, and too splashy in her clash of red mittens and some kind of leggings with holly on them. She was too emotional, especially if she was going to take snapshots every time he acted like a decent human being.

He charged into the thick of the trees, reminding himself to watch for banners and other overhead objects so he didn't brain his son.

Nicki was making him too aware of his own thoughts and feelings. Of *her*. He had long ago mastered the art of ignoring his attraction to beautiful women. Karen's abrupt rejection had made him wary of dating again. Since then, he'd only done it intermittently, aware that relationships were complicated at the best of times. This was the worst. The last thing he needed right now was romance.

With his son's *nanny*.

"Let's get this done. I have work to finish at home."

NICKI MIGHT NOT have been a successful actress, but she'd been a keen one. She'd taken a thousand workshops on character development and was still a student of human nature. She was also the type to believe the best in everyone around her.

So she didn't take Quincy's abrupt changes of mood personally. He didn't like to show his softer side. That was obvious. It was also clear he possessed a caramel center and that Atlas was finding his way into that part of him.

She wondered what had made Quincy so reserved. Despite the cheerful crowd of families at the tree farm, or the recollection from an old timer about Quincy's grandmother, it seemed like Quincy couldn't wait to finish up and get home.

He'd been highly reluctant to get a potted tree. Too much commitment, she suspected, since she and the tree farm owner, Carson Scott, had convinced him to prepay for the next few years.

The tree had arrived home shortly after they did, but Quincy had already been back at his desk. He worked for the rest of the afternoon.

Just as she was starting to think he was too taciturn and really should lighten up, he swung the other way, taking her aback.

She helped Atlas into his pajamas and came back from draining the tub to find Quincy on the boy's bed next to him, the borrowed library books on the mattress at Atlas's feet, the first one already open.

Quincy stopped reading the moment she came in.

"Looks like I've been usurped." Since she and Maury had both done a rotation through those books already today, she didn't argue. "I'll head home and see you in the morning. Goodnight."

They both said goodnight, Atlas gave her a hug, and Quincy waited for her to finish picking up Atlas's clothes and leave the room before he resumed reading.

She went downstairs to say goodnight to Maury.

He was opening the box of tree lights. "You're working long days." He glanced at the clock.

"It's fun, not work. Today was, anyway. And Quincy is reading to Atlas, so I'm leaving now unless you have something you need me to do?"

"Oh, good. I'm glad he's decided to work with him."

Nicki paused in folding the sofa blanket. "Work?" she repeated.

"Oh." Maury muttered something under his breath, adding, "Pardon my French." He glanced toward the stairs. "Quincy might not like me saying anything, but he had a…" Maury waved a hand toward his own mouth. "He didn't speak right when he was little. Sounded a lot like Atlas. Couldn't say his Rs. My wife had trouble with it, too. I didn't even know it was anything. I mean, I traveled so much and figured all little kids took some time to say their words properly. But Quincy was still missing his Rs and Ls when he went to school. I guess you'd call it an impediment. It certainly turned into one for him." He looked toward the stairs again.

She had noticed Atlas still rounded his words, but she'd had the same mindset—that it would sort itself out in due time.

"Do you think Atlas is self-conscious? Is that why he doesn't talk very much?" That had to be why Quincy was so close-mouthed, not that she would have guessed if Maury hadn't told her.

Maury scratched the top of his head. "I couldn't say. Quincy—and my wife, too—they're a quiet breed to start with. Not like you and me," he added ruefully.

"Am I chatty?" Nicki said with mock surprise, then confided, "I sat alone in detention so many times for talking in class. It really was the worst punishment anyone could devise for me. If a teacher sat in to supervise, I wound up pulling her into conversation. I can't help myself!"

Maury chuckled. "I'm much the same." Then he shook his head, growing sober. "Quincy was pulled out of class, too. He wouldn't talk at all. Or the teacher claimed she couldn't understand him. He was sent for special help—the kiss of death for any child in those days. Then he acted out because he was being teased." Maury sighed. "I should have done more, but I left it to my wife. Like I said, I traveled. *I* didn't have a problem understanding him, and we were happy at home. It just didn't seem like an issue to me. But it was. He had to change schools a few times. She tried to tell me, but I didn't listen."

Maury looked so dejected, so regretful.

This was the source of his desire for a do-over. He wanted to help Atlas before the little boy went through what Quincy had struggled to overcome.

"How did you meet your wife?" She moved to sit on the chair across from him.

"Work. She was the prettiest girl in the typing pool, but she wouldn't talk to anyone. So I talked to her. Still do, if you want the truth." He winked, but his eyes gleamed with old sorrow.

"I bet you do," Nicki said wistfully, entranced by the idea of eternal love. "It's too bad she didn't meet Atlas."

"It is," Maury agreed with a somber nod. "But at least she showed me the way. And you're here to help. We need your energy and excitement, you know. I could never drag Quincy out for a sleigh ride, but you managed it." He nodded approval. "Keep doing what you're doing."

She leaned forward. "I was thinking of adding, 'Take cookies to the neighbors' to the calendar, as a way to, you know, help you introduce yourselves. But I'm afraid he'll fire me."

"He might." Maury nodded, then smirked. "But I'll rehire you. Do it."

December 7th

QUINCY DIDN'T KNOW what was wrong with him. He'd spent an hour sitting on a child-sized chair earlier this week, painting peanut butter into the petals of a pinecone, then rolling it in birdseed, while his father and Nicki had gone to the health clinic. He'd been the only man in the room full of moms and tots, surrounded by the chaos of chatter and crying babies.

Atlas seemed to like standing at the window to watch the birds come and go, though, so Quincy was glad to know how to do it. They could make more all through winter, here in the kitchen, where he could hear himself think.

The snow globe workshop didn't sound as practical, though, so when Nicki said she wanted to sign Atlas up to make one, Quincy opened his mouth to refuse.

Then he thought of Atlas trying to see the motor under the carousel. He had listened attentively when Quincy had pulled up some schematics and explained how it worked. He figured putting together a snow globe was a simple way to show him how something else was made, so he said, "Fine."

Yesterday, Santa's slave driver had given him pen and paper and asked him to sit with Atlas to write his letter to the man in red. Quincy had felt like a bit of a jerk, lying to a gullible boy about a stranger who would bring presents into the house while they slept, but Atlas was highly in favor of Rudolf landing on the roof, so Quincy felt compelled to go along with the ruse.

Atlas didn't really understand the concept of a letter to Santa, taxing Quincy's ability to explain the fine line between wishful dreaming and being greedy. Quincy had tried to encourage charitable thoughts, explaining Atlas could ask for Pops to get a new sweater or his other grandparents to have something they might like.

Atlas soon figured out that part. He wanted Santa to bring Lucy new crayons.

"That's the spirit," Quincy told him, then Quincy went directly to his computer and one-clicked everything his son had asked for.

He knew it was spoiling, especially since a box had arrived from Karen's parents, and his father was also hiding parcels in a closet, but Quincy was making up for the Christmases he'd missed. That did *not* make him sentimental. Just a good provider.

Today was home décor day, he noted as he came into the kitchen, needing an afternoon coffee. Nicki had Atlas pasting strips of construction paper into circles, forming a chain. Chipped-up paper—possibly the most asymmetrical and, dare he say unrecognizable, snowflakes ever—were taped to the kitchen window.

"Show your dad," Nicki prompted Atlas as she pulled cookie sheets from the oven.

The heady aroma of ginger and cinnamon filled the air. Quincy couldn't help glancing hopefully toward the trays, but he saw they were big squares of baked, brown dough. Walls for the gingerbread house, he assumed. He snuck a shortbread from the tin while he watched Atlas stand on his chair and hold up his paper chain. The tails rustled and fell to puddle on the floor. It was easily ten feet long.

Quincy nodded. "That's a lot of work."

"If he doesn't lose interest, that one is going on the stairs. We'll make another for the tree."

Clutter and random splashes of color went directly against Quincy's base instinct for clean design and function over form. At the same time, Atlas wore such a look of pride, Quincy could only say, "Sounds great."

He started a fresh pot of coffee, asking Nicki, "Are you having some?"

"No thanks, but on the topic of trees, Atlas said you showed him how to draw a tree with your computer. Can you finish making ours for the calendar?" She nodded at the clean sheet of cardboard that had been leaning behind the kitchen table for a week.

Could he dig deeper the pit of frivolity into which he was being pushed?

Who was he kidding? He was already there.

"Of course." He met his son's gaze. "Do you want to help?"

Atlas nodded. Nicki came around to close the glue stick while Quincy grabbed the cardboard. Atlas followed him into the dining room.

Pops still had the dining table he and Quincy's mother had purchased when they married. It was currently being used as a catch all for Christmas decorations and wrapping paper, as well as whatever empty boxes accumulated as unpacking continued, plus any toys Nicki had picked up when she had run the vacuum yesterday.

Quincy settled Atlas on a chair and cleared off the table while he waited for the drawing they'd made yesterday to print onto single sheets of paper. Then he explained how they were going to cut out each piece, arrange them on the cardboard, and trace the bigger shape of the tree afterward.

"It's a puzzoh," Atlas said, remembering how Quincy had described it to him yesterday.

"A puzz-*el*. Yes." He coached Atlas on how to place his tongue to make the sound.

"Puh-zawl," Atlas mimicked carefully.

"Good job."

The fact was, Quincy could draw a straight line and even some elegant parabolas. One of his old-school instructors had insisted all his students learn everything from proper grip on a pencil to precise lettering. Quincy often scratched out something rough and dirty on a scrap of paper before fine-tuning it on the computer. More than once, those sketches had made it into presentations and other meetings. He was confident he could have drawn a symmetrical tree freehand, but the exercise of showing his son how computer design translated to the real world had been an indulgence of his inner nerd.

Atlas had been curious enough to make it worth the effort, and the boy had a good eye. They'd run through a few options of tall, skinny trees and short, bushy ones. Atlas had chosen the same one Quincy would have picked.

While a voice in the back of his head urged Quincy to hurry the process, telling him he ought to be doing real work, there was something enormously satisfying in allowing Atlas the time to work through the process. Quincy hated to be rushed himself, so it felt good to treat his son the way he liked to be treated.

Now Quincy had time to cut out each bough while Atlas picked up the pieces of the tree and set them randomly on the cardboard.

"There's a trick," Quincy said. "See this one? That's the picture we made on my computer yesterday. Remember I said the numbers would help us put the puzzle together? Do you know your numbers?"

Atlas knew up to ten. Soon, the paper tree filled the cardboard.

"You were gone so long I thought you'd gone back to the

tree farm for a real one," Nicki said, bringing in a cup of the coffee Quincy had made. It was already doctored with a splash of milk.

"Thanks." He tried to think if a woman had ever brought him coffee before. It was only coffee. Why did it seem so significant? So nice?

"That," she declared, "is the best Advent calendar tree I've ever seen."

"Of all the *one* you've seen?" Quincy murmured into his coffee, trying to keep things light. Trying not to be overly proud of a kindergarten project.

"Shh." She winked at him, giving him that little kick in his blood he was really trying not to feel.

At least she was only here for another sixteen days or so.

He sobered. Suddenly, the countdown to Christmas had a different connotation. Not anticipatory, but…

"What's wrong?" Her smile faded.

"Nothing."

"You were frowning. Not happy with the tree?"

He wasn't. Was he? He'd noticed 'ice skating' among the sticky notes on the kitchen wall this morning. He'd taken to checking the wall while he ate his cereal of bunched oats and dry strawberries with Atlas. Skating didn't sound too bad, but there was also 'tea with Santa' and a *pageant*. What sort of mingling with the natives did that involve?

"The tree is almost finished. I just have to trace it, then I'll use a straight blade to cut it out. I'll do that in the garage."

"Then you can paint it," she told Atlas. "How about something to eat while you wait? It's time for Pops' snack. I cut up some veggies and cheese. Will you go see if he's still on the phone? If he's finished talking to his friend, you can tell him it's time to eat."

Quincy glanced at his watch, not realizing how much time had flown by while he'd been working on the tree with Atlas.

"How are his levels?" Quincy asked as Atlas scooted off his chair and left to go upstairs. Quincy had been meaning to glance over his father's pump log himself.

"Everything has been much better the last couple of days. I think with the move and… Well, I can imagine you've all been under stress as you adjust."

Quincy saw curiosity in her eyes, but knowledge, too. He instinctively withdrew, mouth tightening. He reached to make a tiny adjustment with one limb of the tree, but felt her gaze on him, trying to lock-pick his mind.

"I didn't mean to…" Nicki started to say, then turned up her palm. "It's just your father told me you didn't know about Atlas—"

"I wish he hadn't." Quincy relived the judgmental stares as the news had made the rounds at work.

He'd had to tell a few people. HR for instance, and the president, when he asked if he could work remotely. He thought everyone he'd told had been trustworthy, but by the time he had left, everyone had been sending him sideways looks.

"The reason I moved here was so I wouldn't have to make explanations to strangers."

Her shoulders went back and her ever-present smile dried up. "I was hoping you were seeing me as a friend, but okay. I'm sorry. I wasn't trying to pry."

Now he'd hurt her feelings. He could see it in the way she tried to pretend she *wasn't* hurt, lifting her chin and pressing her lips flat, avoiding his gaze as she swept it across this ridiculous tree she had him making.

The tree that was forcing him to spend time with his son—in a good way. As much as he was mentally disparaging these little activities of hers, he was glad to have something to do with Atlas. It wasn't like he could get to know him over a beer.

Every time he showed Atlas some little thing, he thought of all his own father had taught him. Eventually, he would cycle through all those other bigger lessons, too. The proper way to hold a football, how to keep tools organized, and why it was important to be honest, especially with yourself.

"I'm embarrassed," he admitted, frustration tightening his tone. It came with a helping of shame.

Her lashes came up.

It was his turn to look away before he met the sticky dark gold of her gaze.

"Because you weren't married? That's not uncommon."

"Because I don't know why she got pregnant. Whether it was accidental or on purpose. Her parents seem to think it was intentional, but she didn't seem like a manipulative or dishonest person." He scratched his fingers through his beard, trying to release the tension that clenched his jaw every time he tried to make sense of being a father out of the blue like this. "I don't want to believe she used me to get pregnant, but if it just happened, why didn't she tell me? I don't even know why she broke up with me. I thought we were getting along fine."

That was too much. He hadn't even shared that much with his father.

He chanced a look at Nicki. Thankfully, her expression was not one of pity or suspicion. She only wore a perplexed frown.

"Her parents said she did it on purpose? How did you meet her?"

He glanced toward the stairs, aware Pops and Atlas could be coming down any second, but he couldn't keep this bottled.

"Online." He was uncomfortable admitting that, but it had been a reputable site. He didn't go to bars, didn't belong to any clubs, and his workplace was dominated by men. "I just wanted…"

Someone in his life. Why did it seem weak to admit that?

"I said in my profile that I didn't want kids and she said the same."

"Maybe it was an accident, but she thought if you didn't want kids, you'd be upset? That you might reject him?"

"I *wouldn't*. Obviously." He waved at where Pops was speaking to Atlas, voice growing louder as they made their way down toward them.

NICKI WASN'T READY for this conversation to be over. She was learning too much about Quincy.

She found a smile when she saw Atlas had his little fist wrapped firmly around Maury's index finger.

"Did you have a good chat with your friend?" she asked Maury.

"I did," Maury replied, nodding with satisfaction. "He still lives out on the ranch. His son runs it with his wife and his nephew. They invited me for a visit if the weather is good later in the week."

"Oh, maybe we could drop you when we go to the toboggan party at the Canon place?"

"That might work out perfectly."

"The snack is on the table. I'll be right in." She watched them disappear into the kitchen, then looked up at Quincy.

He was wearing his, *Why are you still here?* frown.

"Atlas is really lucky to have you," she told him sincerely. "Both of you."

He snorted and looked away. "Don't. I know I'm lousy at fatherhood. I'm embarrassed by that, too." His gaze dropped so all she saw was the line of his short, spiky lashes. His mouth was tight.

"Have you talked to other parents? Lots of my friends have kids. Not a single one of them feels like they know what they're doing."

He glanced at her like he suspected she was putting him on.

"Check online. Read some parenting websites. Ask your *dad*." She thought of Maury confessing he had made mistakes. "There's this myth that parenting comes naturally, that if you have a child, you know what to do. That's not true. My father loves me, I know he does, but he didn't know what to do with me. We had a good little run from the time I was out of diapers and before he had to admit I was a girl. I played T-ball, and he was my biggest fan. But as soon as I started doing school plays and wanted dance lessons?" She blew out a puff of exasperation. "By puberty, he pretty much washed his hands and left me to Gloria—my stepmom. Maybe he was afraid he would make mistakes, so he didn't try. I don't know."

She chewed her lip, working through that idea as she spoke it aloud.

"He was pretty devastated at losing Mom and I was heartbroken. He's a simple guy, too. Fixes and operates big equipment, opens a can of beans for dinner, and watches the sports highlights. I know he married Gloria for *me*. He thought he was giving me someone who knew how to cook and braid hair and wasn't afraid to buy feminine products. Which isn't to say he doesn't love her. He does. They're actually a really good match. He would have been lonely after I left if he hadn't had her."

With a sheepish glance up at him, she admitted, "Talk about embarrassed. I'm ashamed to say I didn't give her much of a chance. She raises dogs and gets along great with animals, but she's not a natural mom. She wasn't *my* mom. I was angry with her for that, and really hard on her. She did her best. At least Atlas is open to you. He *wants* you to fill the void inside him. As long as you're giving him time, attention, and love, you're doing great as a parent."

His gaze went to the art project she had forced on him. "I still feel like I should know more. That I should know what's right."

She wanted to laugh aloud at how he had over-engineered this painfully simple task, trying so hard to get it right. It said everything about the kind of man he was, how much care he was putting into the very complex and daunting task he faced in raising his son.

She wanted to hug him, but she only said with a straight face, "People who are naturally smart always think they should know more than they do. When you're only moderately intelligent like me, you expect less of yourself. It's a much happier way to live."

He stared at her, perhaps trying to work out if he was complimented or insulted.

"Pretty women are never as dumb as they pretend to be," he said, then quickly looked away. "Or so I've been told. I should get to work."

"Me, too." She turned away before he saw her blush and read the way he'd made her pulse flutter.

He thought she was *pretty*?

December 10th

THE CANONS KNEW how to throw a winter party. They had a hay wagon ready as people arrived and the bonfire was already burning at the bottom of the slopes. Tables were set up with wieners and roasting sticks, buns and condiments, cocoa, and all the other treats that guests brought for sharing.

Mother Nature helped by providing a perfect bowl where the bigger kids could scream down long hills without hitting trees. A much smaller, gentler incline kept the little ones busy. The sky was pale with low clouds, but there was no wind. The temperature had evened out to merely chilly, not biting.

Spirits were high and the crowd of families and neighbors welcoming.

Liz introduced Nicki around while Quincy helped Atlas make several short runs. Now Quincy stood alone on the far side of the fire. His gaze stayed sharply on Atlas as he came down one of the big slopes with Liz's teenaged daughter, Petra.

Petra dragged her heels to keep the speed down as the toboggan descended alongside Liz's stepson, Ethan, who had Lucy in front of him.

Atlas was beaming, having the time of his life.

His father? Maybe not so much.

"Please come meet my boss," Nicki said to Piper and her husband.

The couple had just arrived on the second wave of wagon riders.

"Quincy, this is Piper and Sebastian Bloom. Piper's parents are my landlords."

"Call me Bastian." Piper's husband reached to shake Quincy's hand. He was as blond and gorgeous as his sister, Liz, and he might have been intimidatingly masculine if he wasn't wearing a baby in a sling inside his open jacket. "This is Isabelle." He lifted the receiving blanket draped over her sleeping face. "Not a beer belly."

"Nice to meet you," Quincy said, polite, if distant. His gaze hung up very briefly on the birthmark on Piper's face before he nodded to where the kids were gliding to a stop at the bottom of the hill. "My son, Atlas."

Petra held Atlas's hand as she brought him over. She was in her first year of college, but looked younger, not wearing makeup and gamboling with the middle-schoolers as though she was one of them. She gave the adults a friendly but distracted smile as she approached, eyes fixed on the bump on Bastian's chest. She leaned close to whisper, "Hi, baby. I missed you."

"I used to be her favorite," Bastian said with a pained sigh. "Now I have competition from all these babies."

"And boyfriends," Piper said with a sly grin, making her husband wince.

"One," Bastian said in a mock growl at Petra. "Please tell me there's still only Flynn."

"You'll always be my favorite uncle," Petra assured him, giving his cheek a loud, smacking kiss. "But my list of favorite kids grew today. Atlas wants to go again." She still had hold of his mitted hand and smiled down at him. "We came over to make sure that's okay?"

Quincy gave a short nod. "If you don't mind."

"Happy to. We're having fun. Aren't we, Atlas? We're racing Lucy."

"She winned," Atlas said.

"We'll win this time, though, won't we?"

Atlas shook his head.

"No? You want her to win again?"

He nodded.

"Mom said he was adorable." Petra glanced at the adults with a helpless look. "I might have to keep him. Come on, then. Maybe we can use the big toboggan and all ride together."

"He *is* adorable," Piper agreed as she watched them walk away, then turned her attention to Quincy. "My parents said you used to live here?"

"My father did."

Nicki recognized the look on Piper's face. She had worn it herself a time or two, wondering if that was really all Quincy planned to offer by way of communication.

Rather than leave him on the spot, she jumped in with, "Maury told me he wished he'd raised Quincy here. I'm biased, being from a small town myself, but I think Marietta is a great place for a family. I'll guess that you both agree since your husband probably misses the sunshine in California."

"We do love it here. But are you going to stay?" Piper asked Nicki. "Mom said you were only renting until Christmas and going back to Glacier Creek for the holidays. What about after that?"

"I'm spending Christmas with my dad and stepmom, yes. Then it depends on where I find work. I'm only looking in Montana for now. Jacqui said there was an outreach clinic looking for home support workers in Kalispell. I'm going to check that out."

That sparked a conversation about Jacqui.

"She's engaged!" Nicki told her. "I was so surprised to hear that when, you know, she just lost Russ last year. I don't know her fiancé. He moved to Glacier Creek after I left. I don't go back much, but he's a smoke jumper. That has to be scary for her, after the way Russ died, but she sounds really happy."

"Vin, right? We met him when we were there in the

spring." Piper's voice was warm with approval. "He seemed like a sweetheart. I thought he was her boyfriend, but she said there was nothing going on between them, that they were just friends. I knew there was something, though. You can tell when a couple has chemistry." Her gaze flicked to Quincy and came back to Nicki's with a shade of smug amusement.

No. Really. Nicki felt her cheeks warm and feared she'd somehow given away her attraction toward her boss. *Seriously. Nothing,* she wanted to insist, but held back from acknowledging the suspicion.

Piper drew her over to meet one of her friends, Skye, who arrived on horseback from the ranch next door, doubling with her husband, who was none other than Chase Goodwin, the professional baseball player Maury had mentioned. Chase *had* grown up here, and even though he had to be as rich as any top professional athlete, he was as down to earth as they came.

Not long after, Bastian stole Piper to feed Isabelle. Nicki made her way back to where Quincy stood alone again.

"Are you hating this?" she asked him.

"No." He frowned. "Why?"

"I don't know. I get the impression you don't like meeting new people."

"Atlas is having fun."

Nice dodge.

"He is," she agreed, looking at the smile that hadn't left

the boy's ruddy face.

"You like meeting new people," he observed.

"I do." She couldn't deny it, but wondered if he disapproved. She searched his expression.

"Why?" he repeated, more as a joke, she thought, and it did make her sputter a light laugh.

"I don't know. I guess I'm an extrovert. Even before I wanted to act, I liked meeting people and hearing about their lives. It always seemed so much more exciting than my tiny life in a tiny trailer in a tiny town. Then I realized there was a job where you could take on other personas and live a completely different life, never having to commit fully to one track. You could change your mind and be someone else if you wanted to. It seemed ideal."

He eyed her, his brows pulled together. "A coping strategy for your grief over losing your mother?"

"Pretty transparent, huh?"

He shrugged. "Was it a secret? Do you have any?"

She suspected he was teasing her for being a chatterbox, but she found herself admitting, "Failure."

His dark gaze swept back to hers.

"Why do you think I'm so determined to make this little family of yours work? If I don't succeed at this new career, I'll be a very big loser indeed."

"Is that what we are? A project you have to complete for a gold star?" Beneath his neutral exterior, he turned to granite.

"No," she said firmly. "Not at all. I identify too strongly with Atlas to be that cavalier. But I do want to…" She drew a breath and slowly exhaled as she tried to put her thoughts together. "I want to leave knowing that I helped you. Which is arrogant, now that I hear it said aloud. You and Atlas will work out your relationship one way or another. It's between you regardless. But I would still like to think I—"

"Played a part?" he cut in.

She started to agree, but saw a flash of something in his expression. A smirk tilted one corner of his mouth.

"Was that a *pun*? A joke? You finally unpacked the box with your sense of humor in it?"

"It was labeled 'Stuff I don't use'. I forgot I owned one."

That did make her laugh, openly and with great enjoyment.

He barely cracked a smile and kept his gaze on his son, but his expression softened. The big goof ball.

She folded her arms so she wouldn't throw them around him in a giant hug of exuberance, worked on collecting herself, then felt as though she vibrated simply because she stood next to him, aligned beside him. She didn't let herself smile like a world-class fool, but she wanted to.

She stared across the tableau of winter fun, pockets of people mingling, children's bright clothing streaking down the runnels cut into the snow. The edges of the hilltops looked like they were cut from pale blue construction paper and pasted onto the flat, dove-gray sky. Fire smoke rose in a lazy stream, painting the air with the scent of roasting wieners and marshmallows. Laughter rang out with squeals and the hum of conversation.

It was one of those moments in life that were too perfect and made her a teensy bit melancholy. She felt like she was on a movie set, the first big production of her life. And since this wasn't *really* her life, she felt like a walk-on extra who wouldn't have any lines and wouldn't return despite the fact it was an ongoing series.

She might be playing a part, but it was a very, very small one.

Her heart clenched.

"I was taking myself too seriously anyway," she said, giving a kick of her toe into the snow, hearing the constriction in her voice. "It's good you made me laugh it off."

For a moment, he said nothing, just stood there as unmoving and isolated as one of the carved mountains looming over them.

"You are helping." His tone was quiet. He didn't look at her, but the sincerity in his voice reached into her and pinged her heart.

She still felt small and wistful and temporary.

QUINCY SAW NICKI'S point about library books. This recent batch was only a couple of days old, but he was already thinking of taking Atlas into town to choose some fresh ones.

He had taken over story time because he'd been worried about his son's ability to enunciate, but now it was one of his favorite things to do with the boy. Quincy wasn't demonstrative or affectionate by nature, but feeling his son's small body resting against his was strangely satisfying. The bedtime ritual always made him feel like he'd made it through another day as a parent. The boy was safe, well fed, and as content as he could manage.

And even though he mostly read and Atlas mostly listened, they wound up talking about the characters in the different books. They worked on identifying colors and letters. Atlas was a little sponge. It made Quincy inordinately proud to see him learning.

He worked on exercises with him, too, on how to say the sounds of the letters properly. The old elocution lessons were so ingrained in him, he easily remembered how to explain the ways to exaggerate the sounds. How to talk like a pirate. How to *leave* and *leap* and *l-l-l-lay* down.

None of that happened tonight. The fresh air and exertion of the day at the ranch had Atlas going lights out between Quincy tucking him in and turning from gathering the books off the shelf.

It never ceased to amaze him how small Atlas was.

Quincy stood there with the books in his hands, taking it in. Atlas wasn't too small for his age. He had looked it up online, then checked the boy's weight and height. Atlas was cruising right in the middle of the spectrum, but Quincy hadn't been around a lot of young kids since leaving grade school. It made Atlas seem almost magical, being a perfect miniature of the rest of the people in Quincy's life. Quincy couldn't imagine Atlas growing up to be eye level, sporting a beard like his own, along with muscles and a deep voice.

He supposed it would happen, though.

And look at him, standing here like the cliché of a parent, gazing at his son with wonder and awe, baffled by the idea of his son maturing into adulthood.

He looked around, self-conscious, then turned out the light and left the door cracked, so he could hear Atlas if he happened to wake and call out. Going downstairs, he found his father watching the sports highlights on mute while he read the local paper.

"That was quick," Pops said, peering over the glasses perched on his nose.

"My audience crashed before I could get a book open."

Pops grinned. "I remember you falling asleep at the dinner table after a day in the snow."

Someday, Quincy might say words very like that to Atlas, wearing exactly that look of nostalgia on his own face.

He lowered himself onto the other end of the sofa and set his feet on the coffee table, gaze on the screen but blind to it. He was assimilating how far he'd come from panic and denial.

He'd read once that the stages of grief were actually the stages anyone went through when faced with dramatic change in their lives. He supposed he was making progress, no longer angry, but still wanting to bargain before he accepted. *If* he was able to help Atlas with his speech, *if* he was able to keep working, *if* his father and Nicki were here to help...

"Is Nicki still here?" He glanced toward the kitchen, suddenly aware of the silence. Her absence.

"She was yawning, too. I told her I'd wash up."

"But she did it before she left anyway?" he guessed dryly.

"You know it."

Quincy would have to double her Christmas bonus. He wanted to tell her she didn't need to do so much, especially scheduling all these activities, but she seemed to like it. Today, she'd taken a few solo runs down the slope, the strings of her pink-and-yellow hat flying behind her half-terrified yet laughing face.

Her excitement had amused him as he'd picked his way down with Atlas. Now he wished he had let go the way she had, not caring how many eyes were watching.

He enjoyed the day, despite his reluctance to go. Strangers annoyed him and work... No, he couldn't keep using work as an excuse. After the initial adjustment of making the shift to working at home, he discovered he liked working in fits and starts around walking with Atlas to pick up the mail or playing a game of Go Fish.

Besides, as the holidays approached, retail picked up and building slowed. People took vacation and pushed deadlines into the new year. In another week, his office in Philadelphia would be a ghost town. He wouldn't even have emails to answer.

So work wasn't demanding too much of him and the strangers he'd met today hadn't been the least bit annoying. Some were on the nosy side, but they'd all welcomed Atlas into the fold of children. Quincy couldn't begrudge them asking where they'd come from and why they'd chosen Marietta. His father's pedigree and fondness for the town had bought him a lot of goodwill.

No, today had been the kind of day he should have had as a child, but they'd lived in the city and he'd been a loner.

It made him wonder what other entertainments Nicki had in store for them. He could see the three-foot high cardboard tree next to the real one, but while the real one was filled with a paper chain, lights, and the baubles Quincy remembered from his childhood, the fake one was empty.

It still looked pretty good. Cutting curves with a straight blade had been a challenge, but Nicki smoothed out the flaws. Once Atlas painted the tree a bright green, Nicki had used fabric glue to outline the whole thing with a strip of folded red ribbon.

She had since glued fabric numbers onto the tree, too, using them to anchor paperclips under each date. Last night, she had emailed him a file and asked him to print out the line drawings of tree ornaments. Each one had an empty box in the middle with dotted lines, waiting to be filled with a message.

Tomorrow, he imagined, she and Atlas would color those drawings. She would cut out the baubles and her multi-directional scrawl would record the activities they had enjoyed so far. The notes from the kitchen wall would be transferred and Christmas was starting to work its magic on him because he already anticipated the surprise of discovering what she proposed next. Ice skating? Picnic by the tree? Family game night?

He racked his brain, trying to think of something she hadn't, wondering if he could surprise her with something *she* wouldn't expect.

"You hear about this?" Pops asked, leaning across with the folded newspaper. His thumbnail indicated a bold headline.

"Hmm?" Quincy said, barely taking in what he read.

From Montanique to Marietta – High Flying Prince Visits Big Sky Country.

"They don't mean a real prince, do they? What paper are you reading? One of those things from the grocery store checkout line?"

"It's the Copper Mountain Courier, same as I had delivered in Philadelphia. That's real. There's a prince visiting Marietta, right now. Prince Theodore David Chenery."

"April Fool," Quincy accused, taking the paper to read it. "Where exactly have you brought me? Narnia? We never had royalty in Philly. What's he doing *here*?"

Visiting his grandparents, apparently. The prince, also a pilot, had taken over something called the Bramble House for the month of December.

"I heard people saying something about this today. I genuinely thought they were talking about a TV show. Oh, he'll be at the ball," Quincy said as he read further, exaggerating his tone of nonchalance. "I didn't know there was going to be a Christmas ball, but *okay*. We are in a land far, far away, aren't we? Who's playing Cinderella? Do the mice know they have a lot of work ahead of them?"

He handed back the paper.

Pops gave him a look.

"What?"

"You know who Cinderella is."

"What?" The wheels in his head screeched to a halt, hanging up on the sharp shaft of the impossible. His ears rang at the mere idea. "No. Pops. She's my employee."

"I'm just saying." Pops shook out the paper and turned the page. "She's doing a lot to make Christmas special for your son. You know what makes a woman feel special? Putting on a nice dress and going out for an evening."

"Then you take her," Quincy advised.

"Maybe I will," Pops threatened, tucking his chin to read.

Quincy stared at all those empty spots on the Advent calendar and silently cursed his father, the Prince of Montanique, and the spirit of giving.

December 11th

NICKI DIDN'T USUALLY swear, but she found a few cobalt gems when her car refused to start. On a Sunday. *Good luck finding a mechanic.*

Throwing herself from her car, she remembered not to slam the door, since it was before eight in the morning, but she wanted to. She was so *mad*.

Shouldering her bag, she gave her car one last dirty look and started walking.

At least the weather wasn't too bad. She was already dressed for the cold, but honestly. She couldn't afford to have the car serviced. Not if she wanted to pay her father back for the tires.

And there went her phone. Of course it was in the bottom of her bag. "Argh."

She fished it out and saw a text from Quincy.

Can you pick up milk on your way? I'll pay you back.

She was perfectly happy to pay for milk herself, since she ate with them, but it was the opposite direction. *Argh and double-argh*. She reached the corner and turned left, ensuring she had a clear path ahead of her before she texted back.

Car won't start. Am walking. Will be late.

Before she could pocket her phone, it rang. It was Quincy.

Sweeping her thumb across the screen as she strode quickly up the street, she said a breathless, "Hello?"

"Don't walk. I'll come get you."

"It's fine. I'm dressed warm, and it's not that far."

"Where are you? I'm coming."

"Quincy, it's *fine*. I'm not going to be eaten by a bear. I'll just be a little late."

"I have to go out for milk anyway."

"No, I'm getting it. I'm walking there now. It won't take that long."

"It's three miles. Atlas, do you want to drive with me to pick up Nicki and buy some milk? Okay, go get dressed. We'll meet you at the store," he told Nicki.

"Fine," she muttered. "I was planning to buy groceries today anyway. I'll start a cart."

Ten minutes later, she was reading the label on a box of crackers when little boots came at her in a rapid *clomp, clomp, clomp*. Atlas's jacket was open, his hair mussed, and his little face bright. Pup-pup dangled from Atlas's wringing grip on his skinny little neck.

"Foun' you."

"You did find me. Are you hungry? I thought there was enough milk for cereal this morning when I left last night."

"There was for him. I had toast." Quincy strode down the aisle toward her.

Why did the sight of him take her breath? He looked the same as he did every morning—and made her catch her breath each time, if she was honest. There was something about seeing him wearing sweats and a T-shirt, that little bit of stubble not yet cleaned up from around his beard. It softened all his hard edges and made her feel like she was part of his inner circle.

Part of his family.

This morning, he had covered his head with a ball cap and carried a travel mug of coffee. He tilted the mug.

"I tried some of my dad's protein drink in this." His mouth twisted with disgust. "Yeah. No. We need milk. Stat."

She smirked. "Check the front of the store. Sometimes, they have courtesy coffee."

He did and came back with a coffee for her along with a loaf of raisin bread. Then he paced her, absently putting things in the cart, occasionally asking Atlas, "Do you like this kind? Did your mom ever buy this for you?"

Atlas rode the end of the cart and helped her pick out fruits and vegetables when they arrived at produce.

"This is a lot more groceries than I usually get. Your dad must be hungry," she said teasingly. "I'll have to let him drive. It's too heavy."

"I'm a sucker for sale tags. What can I say?" Quincy took control of the cart.

"You are the cutest family," an older woman said, stopping her bagging of oranges to smile at them. "It's made my day to watch you this morning."

"Oh, um—" Nicki blushed. "We're—"

"Thank you," Quincy said. "It's kind of you to say."

Nicki was so startled, she could only stare at him as they made their way to the checkout.

"My mother taught me to accept compliments graciously," he told her, handing a box of cereal to Atlas so the boy could put it on the belt. "And if she thinks I look like I know what I'm doing with him? I'll take it."

"It's Woo-Doff," Atlas said, pointing to one of the treats in the display that had been packaged with seasonal characters. "Can I haff one?"

Quincy started to reach out, but Nicki caught his hand, stopping him.

He froze.

Their eyes met.

It was weird.

She let him go, quickly turning her attention to Atlas. "You'll, um—" She cleared her throat. "You should wait and see if Santa puts one in your stocking."

"Good one," Quincy murmured, but they made a point of moving a half step away from each other.

He went back to moving groceries from the cart while Nicki closed her hand over the tingling that lingered in her palm from the contact with his fingers.

"Are you going to the ball?" the cashier asked as she swept items across the scanner.

"I saw something about it at the library, but it's not for kids, is it?" Nicki moved out of the way so Quincy could bring the empty cart through. "Someone told me yesterday that there's a prince in town. Is that for real?"

"It was in the paper," Quincy said. "It must be true."

"It is," the cashier assured him. "He's supposed to be at the ball, too, so definitely formal and for adults only. Even without the prince, it was looking like a great date night. I told my husband we're going for *sure*."

"I think we'll stick to kid-friendly events this year." Nicki made a point of not looking at Quincy, just thanked the woman and asked Atlas if he wanted to look at the painting on the windows with her. "Who's that leading Santa's sleigh?"

"Woo-doff!"

QUINCY HELPED HER bring in the bags of groceries, not bothering to take off his shoes and jacket. As he set the last load on the kitchen table, he said, "Give me your keys. I'll see if I can figure out what's wrong with your car."

"What? Oh, you don't have to. I left a message with a

service station. I'll ask them to tow it tomorrow—"

"You don't like accepting help, do you?" He folded his arms and cocked his head. Had she really thought he would let her walk all the way here and all the way home today? When she was so quick to do things for his son and father?

"I…" She waved a helpless hand. "I've been living on charity of one kind or another for years. Borrowing money off my dad, begging favors and cups of sugar. I'm trying really hard to get my act together. Asking my boss to fix my car seems really…" She shook her head.

"He offered," Quincy pointed out. "You didn't ask. And I like tinkering. If it wasn't the middle of winter and parked on a road, I'd take Atlas with me."

"Well, if you're sure you don't mind." She went to her purse and drew out her keys. "I would appreciate it. So I know what to tell the mechanic."

Quincy didn't mind at all, but after he got a good look at what an aged tin can the car really was, he made a note to only let her take his Bronco if she needed to drive Atlas or his father anywhere.

"I got it running, but I think it's the fuel pump," he said when he returned, handing over her keys. "Your landlord, Henry, came out when he saw me. He knows a good mechanic and said he'd make a call in the morning."

"They're such nice people, aren't they? Did they feed you?"

"Tried to. I asked them to come by for coffee this afternoon and say hi to Pops, since Henry thought they knew each other from their school days."

"Oh, that's nice!" She looked at him like he'd saved a busload of children.

Was he really such a bear most of the time? He didn't mean to be. He had been on the defensive since learning about Atlas. That was fading, but he wasn't sure why. Perhaps it was the sense that he would be able to find a place in this community, or Nicki's confiding her fear of failure, which made him more accepting of his own. Maybe it was a sense that he was beginning to *feel* like a father.

Whatever was going on, he was in a better mood. That allowed him to see what a miserable son of a gun he'd been until now and say self-deprecatingly, "I have to start booking things I can stand to do. Otherwise, you'll have me caroling at the senior center."

Quick as lightning, she said, "That reminds me. We're putting on a nativity play in the front yard. Go find a sheet that fits." She cut him a look that was sassy enough to warm his blood. "Smart aleck."

He chuckled, entirely too pleased with what felt like flirting. *So* not a good idea, yet he found himself showing her the inside of the cookie tin.

"You didn't bake enough cookies." There were only half a dozen shortbreads left.

"Oh, please, Fingers McFlannigan. You never leave them alone! I've had three, Atlas has one after lunch and your father doesn't eat them at all."

"That can't be true." *Dang.* He worked out, but he'd have to step it up or ease up on the sweet tooth. "Butter tarts?"

"Also gone. But I was going to make gingersnaps with Atlas today. They should be ready by the time the Tierneys get here. Be careful, though," she scolded with a wag of her finger. "A moment on the lips…"

Her pert lips were pink and shiny and the corners curled with amusement. The way her lashes swept up to see his reaction seemed extra pretty. Cheeky. Like she was having fun.

She had a little jug of molasses in her hand and wore a red-and-white striped sweater over a pair of hip-hugging jeans. He kept reminding himself she was off limits. He shouldn't look, should be a gentleman, but there was no ignoring the fact she was a woman.

She was a very pretty woman, but that wasn't what made her so attractive. She was funny, big-hearted, and determined. And, he suspected, passionate. No one went at so many projects with that much verve unless they had a zest for life that went right to her core.

It made her intriguing to him in a really base way. Sex wasn't a sport for him. He liked it, a lot, but he had to like the woman. He had to want to be with her outside of bed in order to want to share his own.

He liked Nicki.

He was deeply attracted to her. Dangerously so.

Her smile faded. She licked her lips, leaving them parted. He thought she might have drawn in a breath and now held it.

When he looked into her dark ale eyes, he saw she was looking at his mouth.

Which was tingling.

He felt the pull. Not a conscious, *Should I kiss her?* It was a far more primal compulsion. *Kiss her.*

His equilibrium tilted as he started to lean in.

The kitchen door swung with a squeak. Atlas came in with a handful of felt-tip markers. "Can I dwah?"

Quincy jerked back.

Nicki swung around to face his son, her profile pink.

"Sure, honey." She cleared her throat. "I thought we'd color the ornaments for the Advent calendar today, but we have to make cookies, too. Do you want to help with the dough or color?"

Atlas looked up at Quincy. "Do you wanna dwah wiff me?"

"I need to oil the door first," Quincy said, voice strangled as he tried to catch a lungful of air. "Then, yeah. Sure. I'll be right back."

He went into the garage and stood in the cold with his jacket open, head tilted back to look at the garage door rails, desperately trying to catch his inner hound and put him back on his leash.

What the hell had nearly happened in there?

OH, THAT WRETCHED car of hers. As they all sat down to dinner, she realized she would have to ask Quincy to drive her home.

She had managed to avoid being alone with Quincy for the rest of the day today—not hard when he barricaded himself behind his computer and avoided eye contact.

Had they almost kissed? He had started to *lean in*.

"This looks delicious," Maury said as they started.

"Thank you." She'd made the roast Quincy had set in the cart at the grocery store. Her skills in the kitchen weren't master-chef level, but she had worked in many cafés and restaurants, serving, bussing, or short-order cooking. She could throw together a decent meal without much effort. Her classes on nutrition had formalized some of her skills and taught her to leave the high sodium and fructose-laden flavorings on the shelf, to use simpler spices and reduce a *jus* rather than stir up a rich gravy.

She should have been taking car repair workshops.

She couldn't even ask Maury to drive her. His car was back in Philadelphia. His nephew planned to drive it out in the spring, so Maury could get around when the roads were clear, but he hadn't yet driven in the snow and didn't intend to.

"It will be good for sandwiches tomorrow. That's what

my mom always used to say." She reached to cut up Atlas's slice for him. "And my dad would say, 'Let me enjoy tonight first.'"

Sitting back to begin filling her own plate, she was a little flummoxed, not having realized she had that memory in her. The men were looking at her. It made her self-conscious. This whole meal felt formal, even though they were sitting at the kitchen table, the potatoes still in their pot and the serviettes off the roll.

She wasn't used to sitting this close to Quincy, his knee one careless knock away from hers.

"I, um, could probably walk home—"

"Don't be ridiculous."

She had thought he would say something like that, but still. "After I get Atlas ready for bed then."

"I can read his stories tonight," Maury said. "Quincy and I will handle the washing up. You have an early night. You must have things at home you'd rather do."

Comfortable as it was, the little flat wasn't her home. It didn't have a TV, either, which didn't matter because she'd been avoiding television and movies, sticking to glancing at sports or the news if Maury happened to be watching, or sitting with Atlas through an animated special. The Tierneys said she could run a load through their washer and dryer, but other than that, she didn't have much for chores.

"I probably have a hundred books on my phone I've been meaning to read, but…"

She liked being here. With them.

She kept her eyes on her plate.

"Yoh phone is ovah daya," Atlas said, swinging his head and pointing his fork toward the counter. "Dez no books on it."

Nicki tried not to laugh, but Maury let out a hearty chuckle. Quincy's mouth twitched. "You can make books show up on your phone or the computer. I'll show you how it works after we eat."

"Your mom never let you play with her phone?" Nicki asked Atlas, realizing he never asked for hers. He was probably the only four-year-old in the country who didn't already know how to use one.

"Phones is foh gwone ups, 'cept I can see Granny on it sometimes."

"You haven't talked to your Granny since you got here, have you?" She flicked a glance at Quincy.

"I emailed her the other day," Quincy said, quickly on the same wavelength. "They're traveling, but I asked what time might work for a call. We'll see if we can do that tomorrow," he told Atlas. "You can show her that her parcel arrived, and the presents are under the tree. Sound good?"

Atlas nodded and stuffed a big bite of mashed potato into his mouth.

This was what she liked being a part of, the minutia of their lives. Feeling like a family.

She had to swallow hard to make the next bite go down

and felt dejected as she and Quincy went out to the garage after dinner.

"I'm really sorry," she murmured as they left Quincy's driveway and headed into town. "I knew that car was a piece of junk when I bought it." She was trying to keep the dark of the Bronco from feeling too intimate.

"The tires are worth more than the rest of it." She couldn't tell if that was his recently recovered sense of humor or the detached killjoy who had greeted her the first day.

"I didn't have much choice." She turned her head as they passed a colorful light display outside a house.

"If you need an advance to pay for the repair, let me know."

That was a decent thing to say, even if he sounded uncomfortable making the offer. Even if it was a bitter pill for her to swallow.

"Thanks." She tried not to sound ungrateful, but she really hoped it didn't come to that. She rubbed between her brows. "I'm going to try to limp it along until I go back to Glacier Creek. Otherwise, I won't be able to pay my dad back for said tires."

"Really? I wouldn't recommend it. It'll probably break down again before that."

"I have to try. I told you I've been awful to his wife over the years, right? Not *really* awful, just... less than gracious, even though they've always sent me money every time I asked. And I've never put them hugely out of pocket, just asked for loans here and there and paid back what I could when I could. I swore to myself I wouldn't ask for another penny once I got through the nursing-aide course. Then I needed the snow tires. I really, really want to pay that back when I see them again. Especially since—"

Why was she talking? *This* was why she didn't want to go back to her empty apartment. She would just obsess about things she couldn't change. Far better to distract herself with organizing a linen closet and other make-work projects at Quincy's house.

"Since?" he prompted.

"Gloria told me I wasn't going to make it in Hollywood anyway," she admitted darkly. "I can't stomach going back there not just having failed, but as a broke failure who still owes them money. I only want it to flow one way from now on, back to them until we're square." It should feel better to get that off her chest, but nope. She still felt like a massive loser.

After a surprised moment, Quincy said, "She really said you wouldn't make it? My father has never once told me I wasn't capable of doing whatever I wanted to try. Guitar lessons even, and I do *not* have an ear for music."

"Parenting 101, right? Encourage your kid no matter what." Nicki stared at the blur of colored Christmas lights against the dark Montana skies. "She thought she was being kind, I suppose, trying to spare me from what I'm going through now. Which of course I didn't see and resented her for saying, but who tells an eighteen-year-old girl to get married and settle down?"

"She really told you that? At *eighteen*?"

"Right? And yes, she did. I was dating this guy, a local boy. He was nice. Maybe if I had stayed I would have married him, once I grew up a bit, but I wanted to act. Gloria said Hollywood was a lot tougher than I expected, that nothing would come of my going there, and that deep down I wanted to marry and raise a family anyway, so what was the point? She told me to stay in Glacier Creek because, as marriage material went, Corbin was a solid prospect. He was. For sure. He worked with Dad as a heavy-duty mechanic, but..."

"You were *eighteen*. I don't know why I'm so shocked. My parents were young, but I don't know anyone my age who has been married for *ten years*. I'm barely ready for a child at thirty-two. Who thinks anyone is ready for all of that at eighteen?"

"Exactly! And there's nothing wrong with living in a trailer park and working at a convenience store if that had been what I wanted, but I wanted to act. I knew it was a long shot, but I had to try. She said I was crazy."

"Following your dreams *is* crazy." They were coming into town, turning onto Collier. "It is. But I don't believe in getting to the end of your life and saying you wished you had tried something, but never did."

"Thank you. I feel the same, but it still annoys me that

she was right. Not just about how hard Hollywood is, but..." She trailed off.

"What? That you wanted a family?"

This conversation was getting weird again. Too personal.

She swallowed, turning her head to stare through a stranger's front window at their Christmas tree as he turned onto her street.

She felt like she had been staring from the outside for years, wanting back into the ideal home with the tree, the hearth, and the love of family.

"Yeah." Her voice came out husky and choked. "Everyone has that on their list, though, don't they? Right after they become famous and earn a million dollars?"

He didn't answer.

"Except you," she recalled with a small thud of her heart, turning to look across at him. "Why didn't you want kids?"

He slowed to turn into the Tierney's driveway, putting the Bronco in park. His expression was hard to read in the muted glow of headlights off the garage door.

"I'm sorry if that's too personal," she murmured, sorry she'd revealed as much as she had. She reached for the door handle, but his voice stopped her.

"My childhood was less than stellar. That's no reflection on my parents," he quickly added. "But school was a lousy place during my early years."

"Because you had trouble speaking?" She kept her tone neutral.

"Pops told you?" She felt his withdrawal like she'd knocked him back a step and the inner man kept on going, leaving only the hard, handsome shell he showed the world. "I wish he hadn't."

"He was concerned Atlas would need special help, that's all. And it's not something to be ashamed of."

He was granite in the gloom. She had an urge to reach out to him, probably should have slid out of the SUV and left it at that, but she took her hand off the door and angled to face him, continuing to press her point.

"We all think we should be perfect, that life should be perfect. Movies and television make it seem like that's possible. Everyone is beautiful there, and all the story lines wrap up. But the one thing Hollywood taught me is that perfection is a figment of the imagination. Living there was like becoming a magician's assistant. You stop seeing the magic because you know where the trap doors and mirrors are."

She looked at the gloves she held but hadn't bothered to put on, blue to her soul at her own imperfections. At the loss of her ideals.

"It was kind of a bummer for me, because that's what I was chasing—the glossy life where no one got hurt and everyone got what they wanted. But life is actually hard. People are flawed. Nothing is fair. I think the biggest reason I was so happy when I started at the seniors' home was that they accepted the knocks that life delivered. There was no façade because they were so far beyond denying reality. Age spots and wrinkles and being overweight with hunched spines had to be accepted. People are just people. It's really comforting to recognize that. It's okay that you're human and you struggled, Quincy. It's okay if your son needs help."

His knuckles looked sharp as the Rockies as he gripped the steering wheel. "You and I are old enough to know that, but his new school friends might not be so accepting. I worry they'll tease him."

"If they do, you'll teach him that people who are mean don't belong in his life. He'll know that *you* love him and won't care if others don't."

He continued to stare straight ahead.

She wondered if it was the 'L' word that kept his expression so hard. Did he love Atlas? She thought he did, even if he hadn't realized it yet.

Heck, she was fathoms deep in love with that kid. He was sweet, curious, and vulnerable, yet resilient and all around adorable.

She started to reach for the door handle again.

"You baffle me, you know that?" Quincy dropped his elbow to the console between them, turning his head toward her. "Half the time, you're flitting around like a pixie, selling Christmas magic like it's fairy dust. Then you act all calm and wise and say that reality is okay. *Accept it*. Who the hell are you? *What* are you?"

"Just a person," she mumbled, trying not to be intimidated by his tone. "Failure teaches you stuff. It *is* a fact of life. You can't let it cripple you. That's all I'm saying."

"Quit saying you're a failure. You *tried*." Now he sounded impatient.

"I *quit*." It was a fist around her heart, squeezing out a few drops of lifeblood every single time she thought of it. "I wasn't good enough. And I'm a big enough dreamer that I *hate* accepting that about myself. So yes, I have to make everything I do from this point forward absolutely spectacular, including your Christmas, so I know I'm good at *something*."

He stared at her, jaw slack, brow furrowed. "You know what I think you did?"

"What?" She braced herself.

"I think you grew up. There's no shame in that, either."

The way he said it sent an arrow into her chest, but it was both pleasure and pain. Kind of like forgiveness, she supposed. It hurt to revisit something that gave her so much angst, but he was telling her it was okay. She really needed to hear that from someone because the voices in her head never said that *at all*.

She squared herself in her seat, trying to figure out why it felt nice to have *him* say it. She dared a glance in his direction, recalling he might have almost tried to kiss her earlier. "I don't know how to take you, either. Half the time you're a grump, then you're really quite nice. Do you have, like, a condition?"

He choked. "Am I bipolar? No. My condition is similar to yours. A life that went off the rails from where I expected it to go. I'm still trying to figure things out. You are *not* meeting me at my best." His one wrist still rested on the steering wheel. The other elbow was on the console. He stared straight ahead. "Not that I'm ever the life of the party, but if we'd met six months ago, or even three…"

What?

He looked at her and she thought his gaze went all over her face, like he was taking his time with the study. Admiring?

She swallowed, realized her gaze was roaming his face. She wound up looking at his mouth, memorizing the shape of his lips framed by the darkness of his beard.

Would he have wanted to date her?

She looked back to the glitter of his eyes. He was waiting for her. Somehow, they were looking across at each other. Despite the near dark, their gazes held.

Her heart rate picked up. Raced.

The vehicle became really intimate. The only sound was the hum of the engine and her pulse in her ears. She didn't think either of them was breathing.

Dating had been something she had skipped more often than tried. For years, she'd felt surrounded by an attitude that it didn't matter what you knew, or even who, but who you were seen *with*. Even the nicest guys could become competitive about career achievements and had run her down for so much as getting a callback when they didn't. Or cut her loose when they had modest success and moved on, while she was still waiting for her phone to ring.

So even though she would call herself open-minded and openhearted, she wasn't very experienced with men, in bed or out. It had actually been quite a long while since she'd even kissed a guy.

The idea of kissing this man, who was potent and intimidating and maybe not at the best place in his life—

"I should go. Thanks for the lift." She slid out of the door, said with forced cheer, "Bye!" and hurried through the gate in the fence.

December 12th

QUINCY CONSIDERED HIMSELF a decisive person. Focused. But that woman was driving him batty. He couldn't stop thinking about her as he helped Atlas glue a polar bear to the underside of a lid for a jar.

He was back to sitting on a child-sized plastic orange chair while they made a homemade snow globe. The woman running the workshop came by to ask Atlas whom he was planning to give his globe to.

Quincy expected to hear that Lucy would be the lucky recipient. Atlas had asked if he would see the little girl here and had been disappointed when Quincy told him probably not.

To Quincy's surprise, Atlas said the globe was a present for Nicki.

"Oh, that's nice. Who is Nicki?" The woman looked to Quincy.

Other kids had mentioned grandparents, aunts, and teachers. Atlas said, "My fwen'."

"A family friend," Quincy confirmed, feeling odd calling

her that. A man didn't come as close as he had to making a pass at a *friend*.

And now he was back to second-guessing what he'd done this morning. What he'd done yesterday morning, when he had run out to see if he could start her car. He'd taken a hard look at what a rat trap it was, then had thought about her reluctance to accept help, yet she'd been ready to buy milk *and* walk it to his house...

On impulse, he'd detoured back to the grocery store and asked where he could pick up tickets to the ball, the one that was raising money to repair the courthouse. The one the prince was supposed to attend.

He wanted to do something nice. It was a good cause. Maybe he'd been possessed with the spirit of Christmas for five seconds. Whatever had made him do it, he'd walked into his kitchen feeling like he'd found the perfect gift for someone. He'd been smug and amused as he exchanged banter with Nicki.

Then he had almost kissed her.

The tickets had stayed in his wallet the rest of the day, practically burning a hole in the leather. *Bad idea*, he kept thinking.

Even so, he found himself following her with his gaze every time she came anywhere near him, feeling guilty, yet hungry in the way a man's libido made him.

He was her *boss*.

Then he had driven her home and she'd been so hard on

herself. How could she not see how bright and kind she was? How successful at simply being a good person?

When he rose this morning, he had spent a good ten minutes staring at that cardboard tree of hers. She and Atlas were going to make homemade wrapping paper tomorrow. On Thursday, they were going ice skating. The rest of the days until Christmas were empty.

Saturday was empty.

Some things in life were a hit between the eyes, completely unexpected. Things like, *You have a son*. Other times, an action was taken that couldn't be untaken.

He had opened his wallet and stuck the tickets under the paperclip for Saturday.

Maybe she would say, *No thanks*. Maybe she would go with someone else. *Take Pops*, he thought with an ironic smile.

He walked away feeling as though he had flicked the switch that could turn on a string of lights or explode all the bulbs.

Atlas was done with positioning his polar bear and ready for the next step.

"Looks good, son," Quincy said, just the way his own father had said to him a million times. "Now we're going to put the water and the glitter in the jar."

He reached to the demo that was on the table and gave it a little shake as he tipped it over to show Atlas—

"Oh, that one isn't—"

Water and glitter sluiced down his shirt and spattered across his lap and upper thighs.

"—sealed." The workshop leader winced.

The room went silent. All heads turned to look at him.

He looked like he'd wet himself. Like he peed glitter.

Laughter exploded in a chorus around him.

Atlas blinked owl eyes at him, as astonished as Quincy. They broke up at the same time, laughing wholeheartedly.

His son looked so happy in that moment. Quincy's heart clenched. He wanted to hug the little guy until he squirmed to get away. Until he had coated the kid in all the glitter he was wearing.

The mishap was worth it. The one with the glitter, and the one with Karen. Maybe he would never know exactly how Atlas had come to exist, but Quincy didn't care about that so much anymore. He was simply happy Atlas did exist, and was here with him today.

NICKI PICKED UP the Copper Mountain Courier from the coffee table. "Maury, are you done with this one? It's last week's."

Maury muted the news and glanced at it. "Have I finished the crossword?"

She found it and showed him it was completed. "I want to let Atlas paint it, so we have wrapping paper. Have you thought of something he could get Quincy for Christmas? If you leave it to me, I'm going to let him buy the most outrageous tie, just because I think it would be hilariously cliché. But it would probably be better if you and I took Atlas together. Could we go into town tomorrow and see what we find?"

"Tomorrow…" Maury lifted his chin in preparation for making a great announcement. "I have a date."

Nicki gasped with deliberate drama and bracketed her face with splayed hands, quickly lowering herself to sit across from him. "*Do you*. With whom, may I ask? Where are you going? Will you be out past curfew?" She tucked her hands between her knees and leaned forward. "Does Quincy know?"

Maury smirked, coloring a little as he shook his head, amused. "I only set it up this morning. That was Joan on the phone a little while ago, returning my call. Joan Entwhistle, Bill's sister. We're having pie and coffee at the Mainstreet Diner, after we watch *It's A Wonderful Life* on matinee at the cinema."

"Well! That does sound fun. I'm tickled for you." She was envious. But very happy to see him glow with such embarrassed pleasure. "We'll shop later in the week, then. Maybe Saturday? Gosh, time is flying. Christmas will be here before we know it."

"*You* have a date on Saturday," Maury said, nodding toward the Advent calendar.

"What?" She snapped her head around to see something

poking from the paperclip under the number seventeen. She hadn't even looked at the calendar today.

"Atlas asked me this morning what that said. He's quite taken with that thing, you know. He's been waiting for snow-globe day. Didn't know what a snow globe was, only that Quincy was going to take him to make something again. I can't thank you enough for all that you're doing for him."

Atlas or Quincy?

Her stomach contracted with sharp nostalgia as she moved toward the cardboard tree. It was the childhood excitement of a surprise and the painfully real self-consciousness of receiving a gift from an unexpected source. That old calendar of her mother's had been days and days of thoughtful nurturing and gentle spoiling, reinforcing that she was loved.

Suddenly, she was suffused in that sense of being cared for again. Valued. Her whole body flooded with warmth.

She took up the tickets and fanned them. The Christmas ball?

Her squiggling stomach dropped anchor in her toes.

"This is a really nice gesture, Maury." Was she shaking? How embarrassing. She cleared her throat, trying to steady her voice. "But I can't ask Quincy to take me to this. Does he know you bought these? Or were *you* planning to take me?" she added in a thin attempt at humor. "Atlas, perhaps?"

"Exactly what sort of playboy do you think I am, making a date with Joan *and* you? No, I didn't buy those. Quincy did. I suggested it." Maury tilted a sly brow. "Because I happen to know how to arrange the kind of date that impresses a woman. But I didn't know he bought them until I saw them this morning."

"But he doesn't... Why—?" What was she going to *do*?

HE KNEW AS soon as he walked into the kitchen that she'd seen the tickets. She was making lunch and avoided looking at him in favor of showering attention on Atlas. Did he have fun, was he hungry? Could she see the globe he made?

"It's a suh-pwize."

"For who? Me? Really? Oh, sweetie, I can't wait!" She hugged him as she got his jacket off and swished past Quincy to hang it on the lower coat hook by the door.

"Vegetable soup and tuna melts," she told Quincy as she passed him. "Will you dish up for Atlas? I'll run and tell your dad it's ready."

"I have to change. Down here, by the washer."

That made her finally look directly at him.

Her eyes widened as she went from the glitter clinging to his shirt collar down to the streaks near his knees. Most of it banded his waist like a belt worn by disco-dancers. The biggest lump sat like a rodeo prize belt buckle right over his fly.

"What on *earth*?"

"I was mugged by Christmas."

"You certainly were! You have Christmas all over you. It might never come *off*."

"Tell me about it." He hung his hands off his hips as though disgusted. He was ridiculously pleased when she laughed. Why? He hated being laughed at, but Atlas was still grinning. Quincy couldn't get enough of that.

"I think that's your laundry I took out of the dryer this morning. The basket is still in there. Hand me those as you take them off. I'll shake them outside. Atlas, will you go find Pops? Tell him lunch is ready."

Quincy went into the laundry room and left the door cracked as he pulled clean sweats and a T-shirt from the basket. Then he took the coward's way out and spoke from behind the door as he shed his clothes.

"If you don't want to go…" Was he starting to blush? How old was he? "I just wanted to thank you for your help with Atlas."

It was true, but her silence was deafening. Was she even there?

"And I figured, when are we likely to rub elbows with royalty again?" He stepped into his track pants and tied them off. "But if you think it's crossing a line because I'm your boss—?"

"No!" Her voice sounded kind of high.

He stood there, shirtless, holding the clean one, straining to hear her.

"I mean, it's really thoughtful. I just… Like, do you want

to see this prince then? Is that why?"

He couldn't care less about meeting a prince, but he said, "Sure. Why not?" He pulled his T-shirt over his head.

"So it's not a *date* date. It's just a night out."

Did she sound relieved?

"Sure. Call it a staff party." He frowned. He barely endured those things. Deep in his gut, he wished this could be a date date.

He opened the door, glitter-covered clothes balled in his arm.

She widened her eyes, obviously not expecting him to barge out like this. Her gaze hung up at his forehead. "It really isn't going to come off. It's in your hair and beard now."

He gave his hair and chin a ruffle, but accepted he would sparkle like a unicorn for days. " 'Tis the season of magic."

Her smile faded into something shy. She tucked her hair behind her ear. "Well, if it's a job perk, then sure. Okay. Thanks. It sounds like fun. The ball, I mean. Not, um, the magic."

Her cheeks went from pink to red, but his father and Atlas came in. The worst of the awkwardness passed.

December 15th

"DO YOU HAVE something to wear?" Quincy asked.

Nicki looked up from tying Atlas's skate, confused.

"I'll warm up once we're moving." There was a slight breeze. The sun wasn't throwing any heat through a film of thin clouds, but she already wore gloves and a hat as well as her trusty jacket. She wasn't too cold.

"No, I mean for Saturday. Pops thought you might need something formal."

"Oh! Um, yes, I do have something. Kind of." She blushed, having tried all week to put their coming date out of her mind. "I have a long skirt that goes with anything."

She'd found it in a consignment store a few years ago. It was a mainstay in her winter wardrobe because it dressed up and down so well. She had a handful of tops to go with it and had decided on the demure white one, even though it might make her look like she was there to wait tables.

"Okay. Good." Did he sound nervous?

She was afraid to look and smiled at Atlas instead.

"They're supposed to feel tight, but not too tight. Are they okay?"

He nodded, gaze fixed beyond her on the people circling the ice. A handful of kids were shooting at a goal at the far end. Parents held their children's hands, teenagers held each other's hands, and a dog scampered between it all. Some people held cocoa and travel mugs as they skated, but she and Quincy had agreed to wait on buying any treats until Atlas needed a break.

"Ready?" She got up from balancing on her toe picks and knees, carefully standing in her skates, thinking it had been way too long since she'd done this. She was liable to be nursing a few bruises tomorrow. She helped Atlas off the bench and held onto him, making sure he had his balance.

Quincy was right there, already reaching to take the boy's other hand.

Before they realized what was happening, Atlas released his grip on Nicki, avoided Quincy's hand, and shot from between them toward the center of the ice. He cut his skates in a slippery run, his technique jerky and his gait wide, his little arms flailing in a clumsy rhythm, but his confidence was one hundred percent. He stayed upright, and his speed was heart stopping.

Nicki blinked at the equally stunned Quincy. "Your kid can skate."

"I asked him if he wanted to *try* skating. It didn't occur to me to ask if he already knew how."

"Well, I hope *you* can skate, because I'm rusty."

"I'm Quincy." He winked and pushed off to chase down his son, moving with ease as he zigzagged between skaters to catch up to Atlas.

Really? Another terrible pun when she was trying so hard to keep from seeing him as attractive and datable? And did he realize that making dumb jokes was solid-gold proof he was becoming a *dad*?

She did her best imitation of Bambi, wobbling herself from the bench area onto the surface of the lake. Miracle Lake, it was called, but she wasn't sure why. Were people supposed to wish for miracles while they were here?

With a self-conscious glance at the skaters laughing and swooshing around her, she surreptitiously clenched her hands beneath her chin and dipped her head. Skate blades had cut patterns into the dusting of snow, leaving scratches and scuffs and swirls. She knew the ice had to be around a foot thick or they wouldn't let people on it, but it seemed really thin and clear for a moment. As if she could see to the dark bottom, yet the lake seemed bottomless. The possibilities endless.

Please let me have my heart's desire.

She knew she ought to be more specific, but she was too scared to voice what she really wanted, even in her head. It would be too devastating if it didn't work out.

"Nicki!" Atlas had made his way around and came at her like Edward Scissorhands, blades flashing all around him.

Quincy kept pace with a relaxed look on his face. Enjoying himself? That *was* a miracle.

As they came alongside her, she said, "You skate really well, Atlas."

"Yep. I yike it." He didn't let her slow him down, just kept up that shaky speed skate of his, steering himself around all the legs and people pausing to twirl. He even avoided a collision with an older boy chasing a puck.

Nicki found it terrifying to watch, but Quincy stuck within arm's reach of the boy, his athleticism worth watching as Atlas took an unexpected path, forcing Quincy to make a quick stop that sprayed a fan of snow so he could change directions and stay close.

She stuck to the outside of the gyration, pushing herself in a slow glide on one foot, more like riding a scooter than skating.

"Do you want us to hold your hands?" Quincy teased as they came up behind her again.

Yes.

"I don't want to hold you back. You obviously possess a family gift for this."

Quincy slowed to her pace, eyes on Atlas as the boy plowed headlong forward. "I ski more than I skate, but it came right back to me. Hey, that's something we should try with him. Skiing. I bet he'd love it."

We.

A funny unfurling sensation went through her middle,

but before she could examine it too closely, he nodded and skated after Atlas while a girl called out behind her. "Nicki!"

It was Petra, coming up behind her, holding hands with a good-looking, well-muscled young man in his early twenties. They were a fetching young couple with their trendy hats, coats, and skinny jeans. Right out of an ad for wherever young folk shopped these days.

It struck Nicki that she was probably only a few years older than Petra, but the girl seemed young, and Nicki felt old. She had never been able to afford whatever her age group was supposed to be wearing. Not unless it turned up in the secondhand shops.

"Where's Atlas?" Petra asked.

Nicki pointed to where he was already on the other side of the ice, destined to win a medal before he was their age if he kept up that enthusiasm.

"Oh, look at him! He knows what he's doing, doesn't he? That's the little boy I was telling you about," she said to her boyfriend. "The one who's in love with Lucy. This is Flynn," she told Nicki. "Goodwin. Sorry, I should have done that first. And I've just realized I don't know your last name."

"Darren. Nice to meet you." They exchanged a brief, gloved shake. "Quincy is Atlas's dad." She pointed to his navy-blue fisherman's cap and dun-colored jacket. "I'm a nursing aide, but I'm helping out with childcare, keeping Atlas busy so Quincy can work."

"Oh, I thought you were his stepmom," Petra said with

an embarrassed chuckle.

Nicki almost said that was her worst nightmare, becoming someone's evil stepmother, but that wasn't as true as it used to be. In fact...

"Does it sound awful I didn't think you were his mom?" Petra asked, setting a hand on her forehead. "I didn't hear you pull out the mom voice, so I... I'm making this worse."

They all laughed. Flynn shook his head at her. "What are you even talking about?"

"Oh, you know. Like my mom is super nice, but if she figures it's time to settle down or go to bed or whatever, she uses the mom voice. Yours uses it. I've heard her. Flynn Goodwin, what *are* these shoes doing in the hall again?"

"Yeah, she hates that," he agreed with a smirk.

"Anyway, I didn't hear you use that voice, so..." Petra shrugged, laughing at herself.

"I'm just here for December," Nicki said, smiling through the sting. "Heading back to Glacier Creek for Christmas. That's where I grew up." Had Gloria used the mom voice on her? Would she have listened?

She really hadn't given that woman enough credit.

"I've been to Glacier Creek," Flynn said. "One of our coaches arranged a clinic to run us through the firefighter stamina training at their smokejumper base. I thought I was gonna die. And they went easy on us, 'cause we were kids and they didn't want any injuries."

Atlas came flying up at that moment, skidding to a stop

when he recognized Petra. "Is Wucy he-ah?"

Petra bit her lips and slid a glance at Flynn that said, *See?* "I'm sorry, she's not. I'm skating with my boyfriend, Flynn."

Atlas's brows lowered and his bottom lip came out.

"You skate pretty fast," Flynn said. "Do you want to race me?"

Atlas shook his head. His hand blindly reached for Quincy's, his dark mitt closing over Quincy's finger. Tipping back his head, he said, "Can we go again?"

"Sure. Let's go." Quincy sent a quick nod to Petra and took up his easy gait alongside his son.

"Oh, he's adorable," Petra said with a little sigh. "We really need to get him and Lucy toget—Oh, hey. This weekend! I'm babysitting my little sister and all my baby cousins. *We* are." She pointed between herself and Flynn. "My other cousins will be there, too. I have older ones from my dad's side and babies on my mom's. Anyway, all the parents are going to that fancy ball. We're going to have a little-kid party at my Uncle Sea Bass's house. You know Piper, right? Maybe Atlas could come, see Lucy, and play with the other kids for a while?"

"Oh, that's a really sweet idea. I'll mention it to Quincy. I think he was planning to leave Atlas with his father for the evening. We're going to the ball, too." Saying it aloud made it real. Her insides quivered with nervous anxiety. "But we can ask him what he thinks. I'm sure Atlas would love it."

"Mom has your number, right? I'll text you."

Nicki nodded, and Petra promised to be in touch. They talked a little more, then broke up as Quincy and Atlas came around again. Atlas was ready for some cocoa.

They sat on the bench to sip it, watching the skaters. Petra and Flynn were goofing around, hugging and spinning together, laughing and nearly falling, very obviously in love.

Would that have been her if she had stayed in Glacier Creek? She hadn't loved Corbin like that. That was the problem. He'd been sweet and kind, but she had believed herself destined for something greater. Not just fame, but something more epic on the love scale. She had known, way deep down, that what she had with him wasn't the kind of bond that would withstand everything her idealistic self had thought she could achieve.

"Momma skated good," Atlas said, gaze on the crowd.

"Did she?" Her arm went around him before she thought about it, sliding him tight into her side. "You must have skated with her a lot, since you're so good at it."

He looked up. His big brown eyes began to swim. The corners of his mouth trembled.

Her heart lurched.

"You know what I think, Atlas?" Her throat filled with sand. "I think you had a really good mom. It's okay that you miss her."

He nodded, chin crinkling, and turned his face into her jacket.

Nicki swallowed and set aside her cup, taking his to set it

away, too. Then she wrapped both her arms around the boy and held him tight.

Quincy sat on the other side of the bench, leaning his elbows on his thighs, his cardboard cup dangling loosely between his hands. His profile was drawn and tight, anguished.

You have a really good dad, too, Atlas. She rubbed the boy's back, tilting her head over his woolen hat, not saying it aloud because it wasn't the time, but she wished on the miracle waters below them for Atlas to see the potential in his relationship with his father.

She wished for Quincy to find it easier to show his son how he felt.

"Oh, Atlas," Petra said, skating up and crouching before the boy. "What happened? Did you fall?"

Atlas hiccupped and peeked at her, shaking his head.

"He's just sad," Nicki said, still running a soothing hand up and down the boy's back. "That happens sometimes."

Petra made a sympathetic noise. "Do you want to skate with me? Would that cheer you up?" She offered her hand, trying to coax him off the bench.

Atlas shook his head, rubbing his hat askew against Nicki's jacket. "I wanna skate wiff my dad." He pushed his hat out of the way and looked over at Quincy.

Surprise blanked Quincy's face. He quickly recovered and said, "Sure. Now?"

Atlas nodded and accepted Quincy's hand to help him

slide off the bench, then let go, determined to be independent while his blades were on the ice. Before he took off, though, he looked way up at Quincy and said, "You skate good, too."

Nicki had to clutch her heart back into her chest and blink back tears.

"Everything okay?" Petra asked, concern wrinkling her brow as she looked from the departing Atlas and Quincy to what must be a very emotive expression on Nicki's face.

"It will be, I think." Pretty sure. *Thank you Miracle Lake.*

December 17th

HER HANDS WERE clammy as she waited at the window of her apartment to see lights cut into the driveway. She had already checked her hair and lipstick a million times. She had scrutinized her velvet skirt, removing non-existent lint. She had inventoried the contents of her clutch to the point the clasp was going to break if she did it one more time.

She thought *again* about changing her top. It wasn't just Quincy. There was a prince involved, so that meant showing some decorum, didn't it? Not that she was showing a lot of cleavage. In the end, she had chosen her black top. It had a mock turtleneck collar with a small cutout revealing her collarbone and a bit of upper chest. The sleeves had little diamonds cut into them from shoulders to wrist. The knit hugged her figure, though, which had seemed totally acceptable for filling empty seats at an award ceremony, but it suddenly seemed too provocative tonight.

It wasn't. Was it?

Oh, she was too nervous to think straight.

Why was she nervous? She didn't want to be nervous. Dinner with her boss. That's all this was. They were only going so they could someday tell their grandchildren they had met a prince a long time ago.

Would she ever have grandchildren? Children? Would she ever marry?

Argh! Shut up, brain.

She started to turn away, to change into the white top that looked like something a librarian wore to a christening, but the flash of light down in the driveway stopped her.

He was here.

A SLENDER SILHOUETTE picked her way down the stairs that led to the door of her flat over the garage. She had told him not to get out, that she would watch for him and come down, so he wouldn't have to take Atlas out of the car to come up and get her, but it felt wrong to wait like this. As she disappeared behind the fence, Quincy opened his door and set a foot on the ground. Before he could get around to open the gate, it swung inward and there she was, caught in the spotlight against the wall of the fence.

Quincy caught his breath.

From the backseat, he heard Atlas ask, "What's wrong?"

"Nothing." His voice had fallen into the base of his throat where thick emotion tightened to hold back any other words he might have said, if his brain had been able to conjure any.

It was cold enough out here to make his ears sting and his breath fog, but he didn't feel it. He was warm. Paralyzed. Spellbound.

She was beautiful, dressed all in black, one hand clutching a silver shawl around her. The outfit was pretty, not too fancy, and all the more elegant for its simplicity. It wasn't the cut of cloth or the way it hugged her very feminine figure that made her so captivating, though. Her beauty was in her warm complexion and the way her rich brown hair fell in waves around her face. It was in the way she looked at him.

It was the, *Do I look all right?* message in her eyes. The anticipation. The pleasure.

She looked fantastic for *him*. She wanted to be with him tonight. On his arm, at his side. She was as excited for this date as he was.

In that second of eye contact, they were not boss and employee. She was not his father's nurse or his son's nanny or even his Christmas elf.

She was his date. The woman he wanted beside him all evening. He wanted her all to himself, without his son and father. Hell, he wished they were going someplace quiet where they could lean toward each other over candlelight and not have another soul intrude.

She gave the gate a little rattle, ensuring it was secure, shaking him out of his introspection.

He hurried around to open the passenger door.

"You didn't have to do that."

He thought she might be blushing.

If things were different, he would have kissed her in that moment, and told her that was why he had come around. Not to be chivalrous, but to steal a taste of her lips with his own. He thought he would die if he didn't get to do that.

"You look beautiful." He gave in to temptation enough to use the back of his hand to ensure her skirt wouldn't be caught in the door. Cool velvet caressed his knuckles, insanely erotic because it was so innocuous. He became one of those Victorian gentlemen who got turned on by the glimpse of an ankle.

"Thank you. You look nice, too." She kept her chin tucked. Her? Shy?

"Thanks." He used a finger and thumb to smooth his bowtie. He'd put on his black suit over a white shirt and borrowed his father's black bowtie. It wasn't a proper tuxedo, but it was the best he could do. He had even polished his shoes.

Not for some nameless prince. For *her*.

He was in so much trouble.

THEY DOUBLED UP in vehicles from Piper and Bastian's house to save on parking. Petra hadn't been kidding when she said she was having a party. Her aunt Meg had twin boys, Piper and Sebastian were leaving Isabelle, then there was Lucy along with Flynn's nephew, Caleb, Chase and Skye Goodwin's son. The older children were also keeping an eye on a couple of young neighbor children who were closer to Atlas's age. They had snacks, karaoke, and a dance party lined up along with a handful of Christmas movies.

"I'm nervous. Are you nervous?" Piper whispered as they approached the entrance to the Graff Hotel.

"A little." Nicki was terrified. It had nothing to do with the exalted personality they might meet. "I'm sure it will be fine."

"I'm sure it will." Piper paused and let Bastian come even with her, then looped her hand through her husband's arm. "You have the tickets?"

"I left them at home," Bastian said, deadpan.

"You did not."

"I did not." He kissed her cheek, then nuzzled her ear, saying something that had to be a sweet nothing because it made his wife give him an intimate look and snuggle in close beside him, head tilted against his shoulder as they entered ahead of them.

Boss, Nicki reminded, dragging her gaze off the pair to the man who was not *her* husband. Not her anything. She had to remember that.

Quincy offered his arm.

Her pulse did a big dip and roll. She told herself not to act like a Regency miss about it and found a shaky smile as she looped her hand into the crook of his elbow, trying not to take too much note of his strong, steady, decidedly masculine arm.

"Thank you for this." She was trembling with excitement as they shuffled with the crowd into the noisy room. "I expect it's something I'll remember forever."

She was trying to make excuses, so he wouldn't guess these jitters were for him. But when their gaze collided, she suddenly felt really, really obvious. His eyes were such a rich, dark brown, and, for once, warm. So warm she began to feel hot.

Someone behind them cleared their throat.

It was their turn to show their tickets.

The Daughters of Montana were putting on this ball to raise funds for the courthouse. The ballroom was as elegantly decorated as anything Nicki had seen in Hollywood. In the corners, decorated Christmas trees stretched toward the ceiling, interspersed between bare-branched white trees shimmering with white lights.

The tables were set with sparkling crystal and white napkins folded like swans. Red and white poinsettias splashed color from the centerpieces where candle flames glowed. Silver and red helium balloons trailed swirling ribbons from the ceiling, so it looked like silent fireworks had been caught mid-explosion above them.

This wasn't the false magic of Hollywood, though. People didn't air kiss and smile with polite distance. They hugged out their greetings, not caring if they creased their best clothes. They spoke with animation, mingling like family.

She and Quincy sidestepped from the entrance to get their bearings. A friendly woman welcomed them and pointed out the general direction of their table.

Quincy thanked her and set his broad hand on Nicki's waist. The warmth of his arm seared a line across her back. Her stomach jumped and she started to lose her grip on her shawl.

He caught the edge with his free hand and brought it up, securing it against her upper arm with a light squeeze, like this physical contact was perfectly natural. Then he nudged her toward where their table number stood on a little flagstaff.

She blindly let him steer her, overcome by a sensation of walking underwater, but the way it might happen in a dream, where she continued to breathe and wasn't scared. It was exciting and weightless and made her feel graceful as she moved in slow motion.

They didn't know anyone at their table, but they were all locals and eager to welcome them. After shaking hands all around, Quincy held her chair, then ensured she had a drink.

She was going to fall off her chair if he didn't quit treating her like such a lady.

The dinner was excellent, the conversation lively. Even the requisite speeches were an interesting distraction as she learned more about the town and its history. She was having a fabulous time.

When the music started and Quincy said, "Shall we dance?" she was kind of stunned.

"You don't mind?" The couple across from them rose.

"I wouldn't have asked if I did." He stood to draw back her chair.

He was wearing what she considered his 'visor'. His thoughts were well contained and his demeanor all evening had been nowhere near as outgoing as hers. But she was learning he preferred to observe the world from behind an inscrutable mask. He was polite, but he let her carry the conversation around them.

As his gaze connected with hers now, however, there was a flash of something that made exhilaration zip down her nerve endings. If she didn't know better, she would think he'd been waiting for the music to start, so he could ask her to dance.

"You see me as a real grouch if you think I'd bring you here, then refuse to take you out on the floor."

"I don't know how to waltz. I don't expect many men do either. Not these days."

She'd taken a few hip-hop and jazz classes over the years, trying to boost her skills to get a few more auditions, but unless she planned to go whole hog for a dance career, it had been too expensive to pursue seriously.

"My parents loved dancing. They were fun to watch," he said fondly as they maneuvered into the crowd on the floor.

"They taught me. Dad calls it an essential life skill. It's been my experience that we hate doing something if we feel incompetent at it."

"Like taxes?" She turned to face him, chest tight as she admired the cut of his suit across his shoulders, the crisp shape of his bowtie, his clean-shaven throat. "I should have asked your father for some pointers. I hope those shiny shoes of yours are steel toe."

"I'll survive." Quincy drew her into the traditional stance.

She was trying to keep this light, but setting her hand on his shoulder was the furthest thing from casual. It felt profound. His hand was warm where he closed his fingers over hers, making her insides tremble.

He swallowed, waited a beat, then they both took a step. Her front came up against his.

"I'm sorry!" Heat flooded through her, not all of it embarrassment. Awareness.

His mouth twitched. "Let me lead."

"Okay." She forced herself to pay attention to the subtle cues he gave her as he kept his arms strong, gliding her into the waltz as smoothly as he'd skated on the ice the other day.

Once she let go and trusted him, they fell into a surprisingly easy synchronicity. He did know how to dance. She swooned a little over how confidently he moved, taking control of her in the most delightful way.

This is how Cinderella felt. Each step was a stone on a

path that led through a magical forest of swirling people, drawing her toward a castle in the sky. She felt graceful and giddy, so happy her heart lifted into a soar.

The song ended way too soon.

"You guys are really good," Piper said, touching Nicki's arm. "I kept smashing into Bastian because I was watching you two."

"Quincy gets all the credit," Nicki said, blushing.

"It's not me," Quincy argued as they twirled away on the intro to a new song. "You're light on your feet."

She brushed off the compliment. "I'm having a good time."

"Are you?" He sounded like it mattered.

"I have to keep reminding myself I'm not on a movie set, it's so perfect."

He didn't say anything, but they danced through three more songs. She suspected she was grinning like an idiot.

They took a break and wound up standing with Liz and Blake.

"You two dance like you've been doing it for years," Liz said.

"You're making some of us look bad," Blake admonished Quincy with a disgruntled scowl. He was tall, dark, and rangy, the epitome of a Montana rancher, comfortable in his own skin and plainly bound to his wife in the deepest possible way. They were the kind of couple who seemed to communicate with a glance, their relationship as much friendship as romance. Lucy was a very lucky little girl to have parents so deeply in love.

Liz laughed and hugged Blake's arm, saying something about preferring a lively two-step, while Quincy shrugged off the backhanded compliment, saying, "That and a dollar will get me a cup of coffee."

"Oh, look. Leave it to Meg to just march up to a prince and introduce herself." Liz nodded at Blake's sister, who was nodding at something the prince was saying, her husband Linc beside her. They'd been at Piper's as well, dropping off their twins, before they all came here.

"I think she was talking to Rowan," Blake said with a nod at the dark-haired woman with the big blue eyes. "She's one of the Courier's reporters. She and Meg went to school together, and Meg has started freelancing with the Courier. She used to be in broadcasting in Chicago and misses the news," he explained to Quincy and Nicki.

"I don't know how she finds time around the twins, but let's seize the day, Nicki. This is our moment to brush elbows."

Nicki let Liz drag her across the room. Meg quickly drew them into an introduction. The prince—"Call me Theo,"—was the most down-to-earth royalty she was ever likely to meet, chatting easily with all of them for a few minutes.

When they walked away, Nicki excused herself to the powder room, coming back to scan for Quincy. She happened to be standing in the same place they'd stood when they arrived. He quickly appeared at her side.

"Dance?" he suggested.

"Sure."

Before they could move, one of their hostesses stopped in front of them. She pointed above Quincy's head. "That's the second time you've stood under the mistletoe. This time, you have to kiss."

We're not—

Nicki thought it, but couldn't make her voice work. Not when Quincy's hand had just curled around her arm and subtly firmed. He wore his visor. His emotions were firmly masked, but that wasn't refusal or rejection in his eyes. It was a question.

Do you want to?

Her heart went into palpitations. She couldn't breathe.

She did want to. She couldn't hide the way her shoulders softened in acceptance, but it was so wrong. So not a good idea. So…

She didn't know if he turned her or her own feet moved. Did he draw her in? Or did she crowd close? Her hands went up to his chest, but only to rest there. His shirt felt crisp. The warmth of his chest seeped through to burn her palm.

She found herself lifting her mouth and closing her eyes, blocking out the mistletoe and misgivings, letting him lead and trusting him—

Oh.

It was brief. Way too brief. The light brush of his mouth,

framed in an even lighter brush of soft beard, was the most mysterious and entrancing thing she'd ever felt. Spicy, dark, masculine. Way too brief. Her lips clung to his as he drew away before they'd kissed the way she wanted to. Deeply. Passionately.

She swallowed and couldn't look at him, the woman, or anything but the floor. What if they realized how hungry she was?

"Dance?" he said again. His voice sounded thicker.

She nodded, reacting on reflex. Somehow, her clumsy feet took her to the floor, but when he drew her against him this time, it was closer. His hand was not at her waist, but in the small of her back. His beard grazed her temple. Their thighs brushed as they moved.

She felt otherworldly after that. Ethereal. Like a spell had been cast. They moved as one, but it was an out-of-body experience. He held her soul—carefully, but it was still the most defenseless, vulnerable feeling she'd ever experienced.

She wasn't sure if she was relieved or dejected when it was time to go home.

He shouldn't have kissed her.

Quincy drove her home before picking up Atlas, even though it meant doubling back to get him. He needed the privacy to talk to her, to make sure he hadn't overstepped and ruined everything.

God, he hated talking. It wasn't just the struggles of his childhood. It was this kind of talking he hated most, where he had to wade through the mire of *feelings*. He had to sort out his own thoughts and articulate the meaning of things he couldn't even define.

"Do I need to apologize?" he asked as he turned into the Tierney's driveway.

She didn't play dumb. She knew what he meant.

"That woman put us on the spot. It's totally fine." She didn't sound fine. She'd been really quiet since they'd kissed, which wasn't like her.

"I don't do things I don't want to do, Nicki."

Silence.

He heard her swallow and glanced over to see her searching his face.

"I'm your employer. I realize—"

"Quincy. It's fine. I don't think you're the kind of man who would take advantage like that. I'm just… confused. I mean, obviously I find you very attractive, but… This is temporary. My being here, I mean."

Obviously. His brain hung up on that word. He worked the steering wheel with his palms, letting the burn of friction ground him. Obviously, he found her very attractive, too, but he didn't think either of them had made that *obvious*.

"Can I ask you something? It's really personal."

He tensed, but hitched a shoulder. "What's that?"

"Did you love Karen?"

He bit back a soft curse. *Feelings*. It didn't escape him that he'd told her earlier that people tended to hate what they weren't good at. *Guilty*. He had never figured out how to love.

"I'm just wondering if that's why you're... closed off."

She wasn't being intrusive for the sake of it. He knew her well enough to know she was asking as a friend, trying to understand him. Trying to understand how hurt he'd been by Karen's rejection.

He drew a breath that burned his lungs and let it out, then just let the thoughts that had been swirling in his mind for weeks spill out.

"Karen was adopted. Her relationship with her parents wasn't great. They're good people, but she told me she never felt like she fit with them. I've thought about it a lot since finding out about Atlas, read a few things about being adopted. I think, if she did set me up to get her pregnant, if she did want to have a baby on her own, then I'm sure it's because she felt like she was missing a blood relation. She wanted a connection that was *hers*, if that makes sense. But I don't know that for certain because she wasn't any more forthcoming than I am."

He thought about his quiet evenings with Karen, their low-key dates, their silent walks.

"I think I was most attracted to the fact she didn't demand a lot from me, conversation wise. There was no drama. I thought we were a good fit because we both kept our thoughts and feelings to ourselves. In retrospect, I wonder how I thought that was even a relationship when we really didn't connect beyond the surface stuff. What to eat, what movie to see, that kind of thing."

He glanced at Nicki and saw he had her full attention. It was like staring down a train, putting his heart in his throat, but he made himself keep talking. "I've confided more to you in these two weeks than I did in the four months Karen and I were seeing each other."

He looked straight ahead again, thumbs working the steering wheel while his inner cogs continued to grind out hard truths. "Did I love her? Not the way she probably wanted to be loved. I didn't see that then, and I feel more for her now. Gratitude, weirdly. I'm so sorry Atlas lost her. I'm still angry that she didn't tell me about him. I'm just glad I know now. I'm glad he's mine. I keep thinking that whether it was accidental or on purpose, either way, she had him. That means she saw something in me worth... I don't know. Replicating? She must have thought I was worth making a child with. That's something, right?"

"It is." Her voice was soft and tender.

He ignored the unsteadiness that went through him, pushed aside his angst, and concentrated on what really mattered. His son.

"I think you were right the other day, when you told him he had a good mom. She clearly loved him. I just hope I don't screw him up."

"You won't. I promise you, you won't."

He wasn't so sure, but when she smiled sweetly at him like that, he believed her. "Thanks. I mean for listening. I don't feel like I can tell Pops all that."

He couldn't think of anyone he could have told. He ought to feel exposed after revealing so much, but he felt lighter. Like he was coming back onto an even keel after the storm of first learning about Atlas.

There was a sense of incompletion in him, though. A need to keep this closeness going. He wanted to hold her. Kiss her again. Properly.

"Can I walk you up?"

NICKI KNEW WHAT it meant when he asked to walk her up. As his feet hit the treads behind her, her pulse thrummed. Her fingers were clumsy with the key, but when she started to push in, he held back.

"Oh, I—?" She had *thought* she knew what he was asking. Now her lungs squeezed and her face stung.

"Better out here, I think." He pushed a hand into his pocket. "Where it's cold enough I can keep my head." His breath fogged.

It sounded like he was saying he found her so desirable he didn't trust himself to come inside. She felt the same, except she wanted him to come inside. She didn't want this night to end. She wanted to touch him. Be naked with him.

Wake with him.

Yearning drew her toward him. It was a still night. The layer of snow on the ground cast a pale blue over the world. The sense of occupying an enchanted land returned.

He flicked open the button on his suit jacket, opening the edges, then tucked her into the warmth of his body as he wound his arms around her.

She didn't need his body heat to fend off the cold. She was oblivious to it, but it was still deliciously nice to snug her arms against his firm sides and slide her palms into the furnace between his crisp shirt and the slippery liner of his jacket.

His arm tightened, inviting her to lean into him. His other hand slid up between her shoulder blades to tunnel beneath her hair, settling against the back of her neck.

She felt like she was melting. Delicious, swirling sensations coiled in her middle as she offered her mouth and he settled his onto it.

A helpless noise left her throat. The contact felt *that* good. It was so intense it almost hurt, even though he only rubbed his lips gently against hers, getting to know her, coaxing her to open, then slowly, painfully slowly, firming into a real kiss.

This was the kiss she had longed for under the mistletoe. It was sweet and heady as molasses, sharp, yet rich, his beard grazing lightly against her jaw, emphasizing their difference. Man and woman.

She opened her mouth further, wanting more of his controlled, hungry feasting.

Time stopped. They were the only two people who existed.

She moaned again, deeper, arching into him, needing the pressure of his hard chest against her breasts, hands digging into his back, trying to meld them into one being.

He broke away, just long enough for their gasps to cloud the air, then he angled his head to plunder again. They kissed for a long time. Like it was the only kiss they would ever have.

Maybe it was.

The thought brought a burn to the backs of her closed eyes. She dug her nails into his back and kissed him harder. Kissed him with all the want in her.

His breath hissed as he finally lifted his head. He breathed a stark curse at the sky, while she tried to find her balance on her own feet.

He was hard. She was aroused.

Please come inside. She wanted him to, but she didn't know how to ask. Her boss. Temporary.

Was he satisfied with that?

"You should go in." His voice was graveled and low.

She tried to catch his gaze, tried to read his face, but he only showed her his profile, the granite expression that was impossible to penetrate.

"Okay. I had a really nice time tonight. Thank you."

"Yeah." He dug in his pocket for his keys. "Me, too." His other hand started to reach out, but he made a frustrated noise and turned to the stairs, tossing back, "Good night," as he descended.

December 18th

NICKI DIDN'T GET a chance to feel awkward when she arrived for work the next morning. She was greeted by a sopping, milky tea towel sprinkled with O-shaped cereal puddled in the sink. A little boy who appeared to have dressed himself because his shirt was on backward blinked at her. Maury was in a suit and tie, hair still damp and face freshly shaved.

"Joan asked me to go to church with her today. It's an outreach thing they do this time of year. I didn't invite you because I knew you two would be out late last night. Although, you weren't that late. I heard Quincy come in. Did you have a nice time?"

"Very nice." She waxed poetic about the decorations, the music, what people wore, and the history of the courthouse. The part where they danced and kissed? *Shhh.*

Quincy came in as she was helping Atlas switch his shirt around. The man of her dreams was looking particularly rugged, hair ruffled by his fingers, wearing faded jeans and a cable-knit sweater that hugged the contours of his shoulders and chest.

"Sorry about that," he said with a wave at the towel. "I got an email, then had to make a call. I told Atlas he could pour his own milk. He said you let him do that?"

"From a cup."

"Oh. Right. Better. Anyway, he's eaten, but I haven't had time to clean up. I have to run Pops out to the church, then I have another call. They want me to fly to Pittsburg tomorrow." He jangled his keys off the hook and kicked into his loafers. "Vandals broke into a job site, stole all the copper wire."

"It's almost Christmas!"

"That's what I said, but I'm on contract now. They figure they can buy my time. I'm pretty sure I can push it into the new year, but I have to try to sort it out from here. On a Sunday." He sighed. "Ready, Pops?"

"Oh, Maury," Nicki said as he rose off the chair from tying his shoes. "Ask Joan if she would like to spend the afternoon with us. Atlas and I are going to finish wrapping the presents. I thought we could have a picnic in front of the tree when we're done."

"What a nice idea. I will." Maury nodded, and the men left.

As she and Atlas were left alone, she glanced from him to the sink and back to him. "Was your dad mad about the milk?" She didn't think Quincy would yell at his son, but...

Atlas shook his head. "He sayed, Don't cwy ovah spid

mick."

"Of course he did." She went across to press her smile into his soft hair. "Let me rinse out the towel and start the laundry, then you can tell me if you had fun with the kids last night."

"PITTSBURG?" POPS SAID before they'd left the garage.

"I know."

"Son, I don't think you do."

"No, Pops. I do. It's too soon to leave Atlas. I know that." A scored sensation ran across the interior of Quincy's chest. Maybe he was slow on the uptake, but he was starting to understand what it meant to be a father. It hurt that his own father didn't see how far he'd come. "I'm trying to get out of it."

"On the other hand, now might be the better week to go, since Nicki is still here. Do you really have to let her go at the end of the month?"

"Her last day is Christmas Eve. She's going to spend Christmas with her family." But he *had* thought about asking her to come back for the days between Christmas and New Year. For January and into the foreseeable future.

There was a very big problem with that. He sighed, glancing over at his father—who was *dating*, as if Quincy didn't have enough to adjust to. He didn't resent it. His mother had been gone a long time. His father deserved some companionship. He hoped this Joan woman did come over today, so he could meet her, but he wasn't ready to give a lot of thought to his father's love life.

Not yet. Not when he was so confused about his own.

"I don't want Nicki to be my employee," he admitted. "I don't want my son to get too attached to her if we're not going to turn into anything, but I don't know how to keep her in this town to find out what could happen between us. I don't know what to do, Pops."

He had barely slept last night, mentally walking around the knotted issue, trying to untangle it. He had relived their kiss over and over, thinking she was the most exciting woman he'd ever met—which surely meant she was completely wrong for him. She was outgoing, leaned into life, and started conversations with strangers just to be friendly. She was like a helium balloon, her buoyed personality and optimism irrepressible. He altered between thinking he needed to grab her string and keep her from floating away, then worried he would hold her back. What the hell could she possibly see in him, a man with a son from another woman? A reticent nerd who lived inside a computer.

"That was the church," his father said as Quincy drove right past the entrance.

Quincy swore.

"In front of the church, son?" Pops admonished good-naturedly.

"I'm trying to do what's right for Atlas." He turned

around and went back to the church driveway. "I realize she's really good for him, but I can't start something with her for his sake. That wouldn't be fair for any of us."

As he parked to let his father out, Pops hitched around to face him.

"My greatest regret as a father is that I didn't see clearly enough what you needed. I didn't take action when I should have. You see too much, but you let *that* paralyze you. Don't let her get away if she's *The One*. He who hesitates sleeps alone."

"Tell Joan I'm happy to drive her home if she wants to come over for our picnic by the tree. And no, I can't believe we're doing that," he added, shaking his head at the frivolity while kind of looking forward to it.

"She's good for you, son. That's all I'm saying." Pops winked and opened his door, waving as he spotted his girlfriend.

JOAN WAS A retired nurse, plump and friendly, widowed with a grown son and daughter, both living in the area. She was so easy to talk with, she quickly eased Atlas past any shyness and spoke shop with Nicki, mentioning she thought there might be an opening at a local group home for adults with mental disabilities.

"I hadn't thought of staying here," Nicki said. It was a bit of a lie. She had glanced at the online job boards and read through the classifieds, but saw more opportunities in bigger centers. "My arrangement with the Tierneys was only until Christmas. I'm not sure they want a renter full time, so I thought I'd move back in with my dad and figure things out from there."

Joan took the other end of the blanket, and they smoothed it flat on the floor. They had already moved the coffee table back, but kept it within reach. That was where most of the food would sit.

She and Atlas had arranged some presents under the tree—the ones she had wrapped from Maury to Quincy and vice-versa. Gloria preferred cloth bags, always saying wrapping paper was a waste. Nicki couldn't argue with that, but where was the fun in untying a drawstring and pulling out a present? Atlas had painted up sheets and sheets of newspaper, creating a myriad of patterns over the newsprint that would give the proper tearing sound come Christmas morning. It would make the requisite mess.

She caught back a wistful sigh, aware she wouldn't be here to listen and watch. She wouldn't see his surprise. She would be quietly pulling at a satin ribbon woven through lace, thanking Gloria for some cosmetics or a book-club title.

She would be wondering, though, if Maury liked the photo she'd snapped of Quincy with Atlas on his shoulders at the tree farm. She had found a frame at the dollar store that said, "My boys". Atlas had wrapped it himself, rolling it about a million times to use up a full sheet of newspaper.

For Quincy, she had found a kit for a coffee mug. Atlas had colored it with special crayons to reveal the message, *I Heart My Dad*. It was a teeny bit cheesy and generic, but Nicki had prepared something else for Quincy.

When the parcel from Atlas's grandparents had arrived, they had included a few keepsakes, including Atlas's baby book. She had scanned some photos of the boy, then took a couple of shots of him in the new house. She also scanned a few photos of Quincy and his parents that she came across during the unpacking. It hadn't taken much time or money to send away a file for printing into a short album. It had arrived on Friday, and she had already wrapped it and tagged it for Quincy from Santa. She left it with the presents in the closet that he would put under the tree Christmas Eve.

"You've gone to a lot of trouble," Joan said as she helped Nicki bring the food into the living room.

"Oh, not really. Atlas and I were having fun making all the food, weren't we?" They had rolled green spinach wraps and red, sun-dried tomato ones around a cream-cheese filling mixed with colored peppers. Once they were sliced into pinwheels and sprinkled with parsley, they were very festive and fancy looking, but not hard at all. Same went for the skewers of cherry tomatoes, squares of cheese, basil leaves, and stuffed olives.

"This is a cute idea," Joan said of the tree-shaped pita wedges smeared with guacamole. Atlas had taken great care to set the pretzels as stems after Nicki had garlanded them with thin juliennes of sweet red pepper.

"All of this was super easy. These?" She took the flatbreads out of the oven. "Takes longer to cook than it does to throw together. Although, I wasn't thinking of Maury when I sprinkled on the pineapple. He shouldn't have too much of it." The aroma of the fruit mingled with the ham, basil, and parmesan, making her mouth water. "Same goes with this cranberry-and-orange juice. I'm cutting it with soda water, but he can only have a few sips."

Joan had brought a poinsettia, which she added to the coffee table as they set out the last of the food. Dessert was a fresh batch of shortbread cookies topped with a dollop of whipped cream, then an upside down strawberry. A final dot of whipped cream on the peak made it look like a Santa hat.

"Best part of this picnic? No ants," Maury said as he tuned the television to a fire in a hearth with instrumental carols playing over the crackle and snap of the flames.

Between calls, Quincy had showered and put on clean jeans and a dark blue button shirt.

"I think I've talked them out of ruining Christmas," he said, hitching his hands on his hips to take in the scene of dark green blanket and colored lights sparkling on the tree from between store-bought, elegant ornaments and child-made craft ones. "This looks very nice, Nicki. Thank you."

He sounded warm and sincere. His sharp gaze met hers, and here was the moment she'd been both dreading and anticipating. *We kissed last night. Remember?*

She started to blush and quickly looked away, urging Atlas to sit with her on the blanket, handing him an empty plate. She was such a coward.

But what if Quincy saw how affected she was? *What if he didn't care?*

Too many years of rejection had made her thin-skinned. It made her try really, really hard not to want anything, to keep her expectations very low, so she wouldn't be disappointed.

Swallowing past the tightness in her throat, she asked Atlas if he wanted to fill his own plate or if she should do it.

"I'm afraid my old bones won't take the floor," Maury said, inviting Joan to join him on the sofa. "Why don't we sit here?"

She did, but Quincy gamely lowered himself to the blanket across from Nicki, Atlas between them.

It suddenly felt like a very small blanket.

"Where's Pup-pup?" Quincy asked Atlas, glancing for the stuffed dog.

"Oh! I foh-gots him." Atlas took off to fetch his stuffy.

"That's the second time he's left him in his room," Quincy remarked to his father. The men lifted their brows, weighing the significance.

Atlas's absence left nothing between her and Quincy except sexual awareness. *This is how close we would be sitting if this were a bed,* she found herself thinking.

Fortunately, Joan was curious about Quincy's job. From

there, they covered all sorts of topics from local politics to comparing Christmas traditions to Nicki's handful of commercial appearances.

"My biggest one was a laundry soap ad. You might have seen it. I fall on my face in the mud."

"I'm sure I've seen it," Quincy said. "That's really you?" He started to reach for his tablet, but she caught his arm.

"No screen time! We're on a picnic. Out of range."

He chuckled. "You're just saying that so I won't look it up."

"Of course I am. I look ridiculous!"

"We'll look it up later," he said to Atlas with a conspiratorial wink. "But that's a pretty good gig, isn't it?"

"It paid the bills for a while," she agreed. "I thought… Well, it doesn't matter. I don't really…" *Want to talk about it.*

Quincy seemed to pick up on that and gave Atlas a light nudge on the side of his knee. "What's next on the Advent calendar? I told my work I'm busy with my son all week. I hope I was telling the truth."

Atlas set aside his emptied plate and went to the calendar, gathering up the handful of ornament-shaped activities that weren't attached to the tree yet. He handed them to Quincy. Then he plopped himself into his lap.

Quincy glanced down at the top of his son's head. "I guess I'll read these to you, then, and we'll both know."

Nicki exchanged a look with Maury, both of them biting

back smiles.

"Let's see, 'Make Reindeer Food'." He sent an inquiring look toward Nicki.

"Oatmeal and cake sprinkles. Some people use glitter, but I'm trying to be ecological."

"Nice. 'Make Snack Mix'?"

"You know, that stuff with cereal, popcorn, pretzels, and crackers… Snack mix. I just thought of it the other day or we would have made it sooner."

"Oh, yeah, I like that stuff. Definitely make it earlier next year." He set aside that one, not seeming to hear the hidden meaning in his remark. Did he expect her to be here next year? Was he already planning to carry on her Advent tree as a tradition? "Take pet food to the animal shelter?"

"That's something Gloria does." She shrugged, sheepish because she had told him how resentful she'd always been toward her stepmother, yet she copied that woman's kindness. "I seem to have adopted that tradition because I can't think of a year when I haven't taken at least a few cans to the nearest shelter. Whatever I can afford. And I thought it might be fun for Atlas to see the cats and dogs."

"Sounds like a recipe for an addition to the family, but okay." Quincy looked at the next one. "Watch a Christmas movie and eat popcorn. Maybe we could change that to snack mix," he suggested. "Mom used to make one with nuts. Do you have any idea where her recipe might be, Pops?"

"I'll look through the books in the kitchen," Nicki promised, liking the idea of resurrecting his mother's recipe. She hugged her knees, wary as she waited for him to read the last one.

"And…" His expression sobered.

"I wasn't sure," she began. "It's something I do on Christmas Eve, but…"

"Yeah, of course. Pops and I always visited Mom's grave on Mother's Day and her birthday, but yeah. This is a good idea for all of us."

Atlas was looking up at him, waiting to find out what it was.

Quincy's brows pulled together in a small wince. He cleared his throat to read, "Light a candle and say a prayer for all the moms in heaven."

"An excellent thought, Nicki. An extra special remembrance now I'm back in my parents' home," Maury said, sounding touched. "Thank you for thinking of it."

"I usually float a tea light in a globe of water. Then I don't have to blow it out." She liked to let that happen naturally.

Quincy nodded. "I'll run into town tomorrow, see what I can find. Thank you, Nicki. For all of this." He gathered the little pieces of paper and gave them to Atlas. "Really. You've—" His expression spasmed again as he looked down at his son, the boy's hair a shade lighter than his. The little boy's expression was so innocent and intent as he clumsily sorted through the papers, unaware of how he was changing the man who held him.

"Is diss da one foh Wudoff?" Atlas asked, tilting a look up to his father.

Quincy cleared his throat again. "The reindeer food? This one." He pulled it from the mix.

"Can we do it now?" Atlas asked Nicki.

"Tomorrow," she promised. "Today we're having a picnic. After we finish eating, we'll clear the table and play a game. But you can put that one on the calendar if you like. I'll show you where it goes."

They went over to the cardboard tree. He slid the edge of the paper under the paperclip for the nineteenth.

"It's ahmost fuw!"

"It is almost full." She helped him count out the empty days. "Then it will be Christmas, and you can open all the presents."

Atlas grinned and hooked his arm around her neck. "Kwissmas!"

"Yes. Christmas." She hugged him back, heart rending as she realized he didn't know she would be gone by then.

December 20th

Quincy hadn't had a moment alone with Nicki since their date. Joan had stayed all evening on Sunday until he'd driven her home. Atlas was ready for stories when he returned, and Nicki left while he was reading.

Yesterday, Quincy ran errands, one of them to pick up a sack of dog food, so they could visit the animal shelter today. He had also spent a lot of time on the phone, working out the Pittsburg issue from afar.

"I told them it's completely unreasonable to ask me to drop everything and go. Aside from the fact the airports will be a nightmare, I have a son."

"How did they like hearing that?" Nicki asked, something in her tone making him cautious.

"I don't particularly care. Why?"

"I don't know. I think a woman would be fired, or at least would worry she would be, if she put her child before her job. It would be seen as a weakness. A distraction."

Quincy looked at his son across the kitchen table, sitting in the booster seat Nicki had suggested they buy, eating his tuna sandwich.

The boy wasn't a weakness. He was a source of strength, motivating Quincy to dig in his heels when he might have gone along in the past, simply because he couldn't be bothered going against the grain. He wasn't a pushover, but he had valued his job and always made it a priority.

Now he kept thinking he could find work in other places if they weren't happy with his new priorities. Atlas wasn't a distraction. He was Quincy's *focus*. He was what mattered more than anything.

"Thinking my career is more important than my son would be a weakness," he muttered.

"Good attitude," Pops said, rising and patting Quincy on the shoulder as he moved to fetch the saltshaker.

"Really?" Nicki said, following to take the shaker and carry it back to the shelf above the stove before Pops got to the table. "I leave it over here because you shake first, before you even taste. Blood pressure. Remember?"

"Bah," Pops said in a playful grunt. "How many more days of your bossing do I have to put up with?"

"I'm going to hide it before I leave. What do you think of that?" she teased as she came back to the table.

Quincy grimaced at his sandwich, wishing he had figured out what to do about Nicki.

"What's dat music?" Atlas asked.

"Hmm?" Nicki started to sit, then said, "Oh, I think that's my phone." She went across to the counter and glanced at it. "It's my agent." She frowned. "Former agent. Wishing me a Merry Christmas?" she guessed as she swiped. "Probably pocket dialing—Hi, Glenda. Did you mean to call me? It's Nicki Darren."

The woman on the other end had a loud, throaty, chain-smoker tone as she barked, "Yes, I'm calling you. With a Christmas miracle. I just got a call from the casting agent for Stapleton Stables."

Nicki frowned, saying, "What kind of call?" as she left the kitchen into the dining room.

Quincy looked at his father.

Pops gave him a told-you-so look.

"What?" He was supposed to have pinned her down since two days ago? *How?*

Seconds later, Nicki walked back into the kitchen, looking shell-shocked. Her hand trembled as she set her phone on the counter and announced, "I just got cast for a serial drama on a ranch. In Texas."

Pops sent Quincy another hard look, but Quincy turned away from it, looking at Nicki. "How? Did you send a tape? I thought your agent let you go?"

"She did, but one of the last auditions she sent me on was for this thing. It was a year ago. They've been in pre-production for months. It's an original series for a streaming service, but the actor they cast backed out. Since I was their second choice, they're asking for me. It's a good part. Steady work for a year. Longer if the series is picked up for more seasons."

"That's good, isn't it?" Why wasn't she jumping up and down, crying or laughing or both? He certainly felt like crying.

"I don't know if I should believe it." She pinched her arm. "I don't even know how—They're on hiatus for Christmas, but I'm supposed to start first thing in the new year. I don't have a place to live…"

"Come sit," Pops said, nodding at her chair. "Let it sink in."

She sat as if she were on autopilot and nodded dumbly. "All I can think is that I haven't acted in a year. Maybe I'll be awful. Maybe…"

"Don't borrow trouble," Pops urged. "This is what you've always wanted, isn't it?"

"Yeah." Her voice was paper thin. She lifted her gaze and looked right at Quincy.

Don't go. He couldn't say it. It *was* what she had always wanted.

Her mouth tightened as though she was trying to still a tremble in her lips. She ducked her head, picked up her sandwich, but only looked at it, didn't eat.

December 24th

NICKI WAS STILL sleepwalking by Christmas Eve. Every spare minute she had, she was making calls to reconfigure her life *again,* this time in Texas.

She would have her own apartment, finally. One that she could afford to live in *by herself.* Being self-sustaining and not sharing a bathroom were two goals she had had for so long, she'd forgotten they were on her list.

When she really thought about it, though, she realized she had that with the Tierneys. As it turned out, living alone was kind of lonely. She wound up spending all her time at Quincy's, preferring the homey activity of looking after the Ryan men.

Tonight, she would drive to Glacier Creek to spend Christmas with her dad and Gloria. They were both so happy for her. She had given them the news over the tablet. Her dad had teared up while Gloria said, "I knew you would make it. You've always been so determined."

Nicki had bit her lip against contradicting her. What was wrong with her that she kept denigrating herself, thinking,

But I'm their second choice. Other people were happy for her. Why couldn't she be happy for herself? Instead, she just felt...flat.

Actually, as she drove to Quincy's that morning, she felt worse than flat. She was flat-out *depressed*. All she could think about was the number of times she had embraced this day as a child. It was the most exciting day of the year, in her opinion. Better than Christmas Day, even. Christmas Eve was when the anticipation of magic was at its peak. It was imbued with infinite possibility. Wasn't she on the verge of achieving her lifelong dream? Her heart's desire?

This was what she had wished for at Miracle Lake. Here it was, coming true.

Why wasn't she happy?

This year, Christmas Eve was the saddest one she'd ever experienced. She dreaded saying goodbye to Atlas, Maury, and Quincy. Her heart was buckling in on itself with the sense of approaching doom as she pulled into their driveway. Her throat felt overly dry. Hot and achy.

All week, Quincy had been acting like their date and their kiss had never happened, which was probably for the best, but it gutted her. Maybe she'd only been here a few weeks, but she'd thought they were friends. Closer than friends. She wished he would act like he was sorry she was going, even if this was the way they'd arranged it from the beginning.

She was his *employee*, she forced herself to remember.

This was a *job*. Nothing more.

Taking a deep breath to gather her courage, she knocked and stepped into the kitchen.

And found Quincy making pancakes. The aroma of bacon coated the air along with fresh coffee.

"I've been replaced already," she said with forced lightness.

"It's Saturday. Dads make breakfast on the weekend, right?"

Oh, it was bittersweet to watch him embrace the role. He was going to get better and better at it, but she wouldn't be here to see it.

"So I've heard," she murmured as she hung her coat. When she turned, she saw there was more on the table than place settings. "What's going on?"

"It's foh you!" Atlas was on his knees on his chair, leaning forward on his elbows, eager to be part of the offering.

Nicki moved across to see three presents, one wrapped in newsprint and suspiciously in the shape of a Mason jar snow globe. Another was chocolates from Sage's in town—renowned for how good they were. She was thrilled she would be able to try them. The third was wrapped so nicely it might have been jewelry. Not small enough to be a ring. She cautioned herself it was probably a tree ornament.

"This is very nice. You really didn't have to."

"I wanted to say thank you."

Goodbye. It was goodbye. Her heart twisted as she looked

at Atlas's excited little face, wanting to kiss him he was so adorable. She had reminded him a few times that she would be leaving to spend Christmas with her own father, then had to go away to work, but she was pretty sure he hadn't really absorbed that when she left, she would really be gone.

She hadn't had time to ask Quincy how he felt about her checking in on Atlas over the tablet. On all of them. Would that be too intrusive? She just didn't know anymore where her place was.

"Pops is getting dressed. Joan invited us for an early Christmas service this afternoon. There's a thing in the Sunday school for the kids. I thought… Well, I thought you'd prefer to drive while it's daylight." Quincy's hand came up in what might have been entreaty.

She absorbed the words like a blow. *Right. Okay*. Not even a full day on her last day. Half a day. Breakfast.

"Thanks. Yeah. I would." Most of her packing was done. She just needed to finish loading her car.

He brought her a coffee. "I really am grateful. I thought Pops was putting the mental in sentimental when he said we should give Atlas a proper Christmas, but acting like a family has actually made us into one." He set his hand on his son's head, still a little tentative, but there was no mistaking the tenderness in his expression as he looked at Atlas. "You're a good kid. I'm proud you're my son."

Atlas may or may not have understood all the words, but he understood his father was praising him. He smiled openly, all his lingering reserve with Quincy gone.

Nicki blinked. "How could you *not* love him? Atlas is *awesome*." She went behind the boy and hugged him, growling, making him giggle and squirm.

"Open yoh pwesents!"

"I'll do it after we eat. But while we wait for Pops to come down, why don't you help me?" She had a few stocking stuffers for the men—a rolled up, large-print book of crossword puzzles for Maury, along with a shaker of salt alternative. For Quincy, she had picked up a pair of the earbuds he liked along with a book of one hundred and one card games to play with children.

They were already wrapped. Atlas helped her tuck them into the stockings, touching his lips when she touched hers, silently agreeing to keep it top secret.

They all sat down to eat a few minutes later, Nicki reaching automatically to cut up Atlas's pancakes.

"I'll do it. You eat first for a change," Quincy said.

Usurped again. She tried not to let it bother her and gave Maury her attention when he asked, "Will you stay in touch? We're going to miss you."

"I'm going to miss you, too," she assured him. "And I'd love to call. Check in on Atlas. You know today is my last day, right, Atlas? I'm going to see my dad, then I have to go away to work?"

He nodded and stuffed a forkful of fluffy, syrup-laden pancake into his mouth.

It was better if there were no tears, she assured herself. She would do her best to hold off on hers until she was alone.

They talked a little more about exactly where she was going, and what Atlas would be doing at the church, and that there was a family friendly New Year's celebration in town that Quincy already planned to attend with his son.

My work here is done, she thought wistfully, not even allowed to take her plate to the counter. Quincy did it.

"I'm going to wind up on Santa's naughty list if I open these early, aren't I?"

"Pretty sure you've only ever occupied the 'nice' list," Quincy drawled, making her laugh dryly.

"You haven't seen me after blowing an audition. Not enough soap in the world to wash out this mouth, let me tell you. Which one first, Atlas? You choose."

He chose his, and it was the snow globe, of course. She tipped it, watching the fake snow rain down on the polar bear and bright green tree.

"I *love* it," she pronounced sincerely. "I'm going to keep it forever. Thank you *so much*." She kissed him.

"I'll take one of those," Maury said with a nudge of the box of chocolates toward her. "The kiss, not a chocolate. I'm told these are the best in the nation, but I don't think anything could be as sweet as you, Nicki."

"Listen to you! Does Joan know you flirt with other women like that?" She rose and bent to kiss the old man's cheek. Then she opened the box, so they could all try one. Maury set his aside, saying he would save his as a Christmas treat tomorrow, but the rest of them groaned and agreed they were the best chocolates they had ever tasted.

It was time for her to open Quincy's gift. It was professionally wrapped in gold foil with a silver ribbon, a sprig of holly decorating the top. Her hands shook a little. She paused to sip from her mug and murmured, "Too much coffee," to explain her shakes.

It wasn't the coffee. It was shyness and pleasure and poignant joy that he had made the effort to buy her anything at all. It turned out to be a wide cuff bracelet in sterling silver, the rugged line of the Rockies engraved in a subtle pattern across the face. On the underside, it was inscribed, '*Marietta Christmas*' with the year.

"I don't want you to forget us," he said gruffly.

As if she ever would.

The corners of her mouth tugged down, nearly impossible to fight. "You guys keep acting like I've done you a favor. This was something I needed so much."

"Don't turn on the waterworks. You'll get me started," Maury warned, handing her his handkerchief.

"I'm fine. I won't," she promised, thinking it was far easier to conjure tears for a camera than to quell them in real life.

Ironic that she was acting happy for the fake life she was moving toward. Living a pretend life had always meant avoiding the pain of living in the real world. Pain like this.

With another round of hugs, the most painful the too-brief one she shared with Quincy, she said, "Merry Christmas," and left the Ryans to clean their own kitchen.

❦

NICKI HAD A little cry, but channeled her maudlin frustration into cleaning the small apartment. She reminded herself she was very lucky to finally have the opportunity to take a real acting job, then finished packing her car.

She was about to strip the bed and start it in the Tierney's washer when a knock on the door pulled her into the main room.

It was Quincy.

Charlie was behind him, tail wagging frantically. Quincy brushed a distracted hand in the dog's direction, but his pensive attention was fully on her.

"Hi." Her voice came out thick and husky. "Did I forget something at the house?"

"Can I talk to you?"

"Of course." She backed into the apartment. "Is everyone okay?"

"Yeah. I left Atlas with Pops and Joan at the church. They were just getting started. He saw one of the kids from the other night at the Blooms…" He waved off any need to worry about Atlas or his dad.

"Marietta really is good for Atlas, don't you think? He's

already making friends." She didn't know what else to say.

"I think it will be. Joan said she knows a good speech therapist. Did I tell you that? Yeah, don't tell Pops that I think this was a good move." He gave the back of his head a scratch, tossing out a half-grin. "He'll be impossible to live with." He dropped his hand to shut the door, closing out the dog and the cold afternoon, then stood there, hand on the latch.

"I thought you were going to the service with them?"

"I was, but…" His free hand came up, frustration in the way he waved it at her. "I don't know what to do. It's crazy to ask if I can call you, right? We're not going to try to do something long distance when you're taking a job a thousand miles away. Are we? That's nuts, right? Because I can't uproot Atlas again and follow you, start over somewhere else. You just said it. I have him in a good place."

She sank down on the sofa, heart plummeting as she did. She clasped her hands between her knees.

He moved to sit in the small armchair that faced it, balanced his elbows on his thighs, and clasped his hands in front of his mouth. "You have to take that job."

"I do." It hurt to say it. Her whole body hurt. Why was life never fair? "It's so many things I've been waiting for. Validation. Proof that dreams come true. I always wanted to believe that." Her voice thinned out to almost nothing. "That if you stick with something long enough, you can make it happen. If I don't give this a shot, I will always wonder."

"Yeah," he agreed. "And we don't even know what this is." He motioned between them. "It's been *three weeks*. I can't ask you to stay. What if it doesn't work out? You would have given up your dream, and Atlas is half in love with you as it is…"

She nodded. He wasn't saying anything she hadn't thought. Except the part about his asking her to stay. The fact he had given so much thought to it made her throat feel raw. All the strings around her heart went tight.

"But I couldn't let you leave without…" His fingers went into his hair as he hung his head. "Damn it, I'm lousy at this. I want to kiss you again." He brought his head up to let the flash in his warm brown eyes spark out at her. "And you're not my employee anymore, so it's not sleazy of me to say that. Is it?"

"No," she assured him with a little smile, then recalled the size of the check in the envelope he'd handed her as she left. "But you overpaid me. I owe you several hours."

"Are you kid—You are. It was a Christmas bonus. Shut up."

It was his too-generous heart peeking past the walls he kept around himself.

She suppressed a smile.

They looked at each other. The silence condensed with conflicted emotions. So many.

She leaned forward, seizing the chance to say something

he needed to hear. "You're a really good father, you know." It was why she was halfway in love with him.

He started to grimace with denial.

"The fact that you're humble about it is the proof."

His scowl turned away, and his profile winced with some internal thought. Then he looked back at her with a reluctant acceptance. He hitched forward and leaned toward her, thumbs under his chin. "I'm still wrapping my brain around the fact I'm his father, and I will probably never know whether his conception was deliberate or accidental, but that doesn't matter. Not in the big scheme of things. I just want what's best for him. That's something I know without doubt."

"I know you do. But there is one thing you have to do for him." She was a heart-forward person, but it was still a bold move to reach out and take the hands of such a withdrawn man. Holding them was an overwhelming experience. They were undeniably masculine. The contact sent sharp talons of awareness through her own hands, up her forearms, and left a tingling wake across her shoulders and chest.

"Tell him you love him," she advised in a near whisper. It was not her place, but she entreated him to do it. "I know that can be hard for men. My own dad stopped saying the words even before my mom died. Tell your dad, too, for that matter."

"You are bossy." He was trying to make light of it, but his hands shifted to take hold of hers, squeezing with something that might have been gratitude.

"I have to get it all out before we really say goodbye." Because after that, she would cry for real, and she didn't want him to see it.

His thumbs moved on the backs of her hands.

She bit the inside of her cheek, wanting to fill the space with words. It was her way to engage like that, but Quincy was like Atlas. He preferred to speak with actions, so she gave him time to have his say. They sat like that a long minute and it was perfect.

Then Quincy rose and drew her to her feet. She looked up into those deep, dark eyes, memorizing them. Mesmerized by him.

They stood there holding hands for another long minute, quietly remembering all the reasons why this was impossible. Her throat grew thicker, her chest tighter, her eyes hot.

Finally, he lifted his hand to cup the side of her neck, bent his head, and brushed a tender kiss across her mouth. It was sweet and soft, filled with every dream of happily ever after she had ever dared imagine.

Then he kissed her again and it wasn't so innocent. She set her hand on his chest, let it slide to his ribcage as they deepened the kiss. Leaned in so they touched.

They both let out a stuttering breath as they embraced fully, body to body, arms going around to hold onto the other. They kissed in short, damp bites that grew into longer, more passionate connections. His soft beard scraped erotically against her chin. She felt him harden against her stomach and pressed herself into him. His breath caught, and he pulled back to look at her.

She only brought her hand up to touch the side of his face, urging him down for another kiss. This couldn't end. Not yet.

They played their tongues against one another's, bodies rubbing. His hands moved more firmly on her, massaging her back and waist. One dipped low to rub her backside.

Arousal coiled in her, urging her to move against him, kiss where his beard stopped and his throat flexed. He moved to open his mouth against her neck and paused to inhale. "You smell so good." He rubbed his lips against her nape, and she shivered at the tickle.

He kissed her again. This time, it grew urgent. Desperate. Neither of them wanted this to end. She could feel he felt the same as her. It was painful. Perfect and infused with sweet yearning.

"Quincy—" She gasped for air, tipping her head back while letting her fingertips dip behind the buttons on his shirt. "Should we…?" She glanced toward the bedroom.

"Oh, sweetheart." He choked out a humorless laugh, firm hand at the base of her spine holding her against the proof he wanted her. "I didn't come here for that."

"I know. But…" She rubbed her brow against the silk of his beard, touched her lips to his throat again, drinking in his scent of aftershave, woolen sweater, warm man, and clean,

Montana wind. "I want to feel close to you."

His arms closed tighter around her. He held her very close for a long minute, chin against her hair. His voice rasped as he said, "I didn't bring anything."

"What do you mean? Oh!" Her cheeks warmed. "There's some in the bathroom. They were there when I got here. Check to see if they're expired."

※

QUINCY LOOKED BEHIND the mirror and didn't bother speculating whom the condoms might have belonged to. He was too busy asking himself if he should use one. Or rather, whether he should make love at all. With Nicki.

He wanted to. So much he had to grip the edge of the sink to cool his head enough to have this mental debate. His body was primed, so hard he was hurting. He ached to relieve the pressure by opening his fly. If he started thinking about undressing, about how good Nicki would feel, naked and soft against him, he would be lost.

He was a typical man. He liked sex. And he liked Nicki. He was pretty sure it was a lot more than mere 'like'. He definitely didn't want anything to tarnish or ruin what they had between them. He didn't want to come across as an opportunist when he was wishing so badly they had more time to figure things out.

At the same time, as he moved back to the bedroom and saw her in the lamplight, nervously leaning to smooth the sheets on the bed, he was not only overcome by pure, male appreciation for a supple body, he was greedy for *this*. This moment that only existed between the two of them.

Making love with her had nothing to do with his father or his son or anything except who *they* were. Him and Nicki. Man and woman. It was something only they would share. It would be a memory he would have for the rest of his life.

That was both disturbing and reassuring. It wasn't something either of them was doing lightly. The shy way she glanced up at him told him she was nervous.

So was he. He wasn't a romance-novel hero. He just wanted her to feel as good as she made him feel. Not just physically, either. Everything about the way she treated him made him feel good about who he was. Father, son, man. It was incredibly addictive. Deeply gratifying.

So many thoughts and feelings crowded into his throat, he couldn't make anything coherent come out. All he could think was he wanted to *show* her how much she meant to him.

He absently set the box on the nightstand and met her at the foot of the bed, stopping her hands from wringing nervously so he could hold her, just hold her. Her hair was soft and fragrant against his lips, catching in his beard. Her body was warm and slight, so curvy and oddly fragile when he really let himself absorb the shape of her. A rush of protectiveness rose in him to balance his sexual hunger, making him capable of gentleness.

Tenderness.

Her breath eased out and she relaxed against him. "I'm not... I don't... It's been a while for me. I'm not having second thoughts, just..."

"Me, too," he murmured, kissing her brow, her cheekbone, finding her mouth and inviting her to kiss him back. "No rush. I just want to feel you."

She seemed to melt in his arms.

He was a goner.

HE MADE HER feel like she was the only woman he'd ever seen in his life as they took their time undressing each other, kissing, lightly caressing, following the contour of a collarbone, a bicep, the indent of waist or the flex of a shoulder blade.

He drew the straps of her bra down, and his hand shook as he very gently cupped her breast. "So beautiful," he murmured, thumb grazing across her nipple. He pressed his mouth to her bare shoulder. "I can't believe how beautiful you are."

She could feel the hunger in him, his strain as he struggled to hold back, making him hard everywhere. He wanted to take his time, give *them* time. It was seductive and enthralling and she grew more and more aroused, quivering with desire by the time they stood naked, skin against skin.

"You're shaking. Scared?"

"No," she said on a gasp as he massaged her breast again. "I mean, I'm nervous, but I feel like I'm going to fall down." She touched his beard, filling her palm with the thick silk. He was so handsome he stole her breath.

They flowed onto the bed, not bothering to get under the covers, just lying atop the blankets, limbs entangled as they kissed and nuzzled and caressed. He ran his lips down her neck. This time, he went all the way to her breast, taking her nipple so she gasped at the flood of heat. Sweet sensations ran into her loins, making her ache at the fork of her thighs.

"Quincy." His nipples were sharp where her palms stroked across them. He was so hard against her thigh. So hot. She touched him, feeling the jerk that went through his whole body.

He lifted his head and covered her hand, showing her what he liked as he kissed her, then he touched her, too, gently parting where she was slippery and yearning. As his fingers drew lazily back and forth, she tightened her fist on him, only realizing she was biting his lip when he gave a soft grunt of pleasure-pain and pulled back, then took control of their kiss in a hungry way that was so exciting she started to lose herself in the pleasure he was giving her.

"I'm sorry," she gasped, drawing back a little so she could look at his bottom lip. "Did I hurt you?"

"It was sexy. I thought you were almost there."

"I was." *Am.* She'd never been so turned on in her life. "I want you with me."

He reached back. Seconds later, he had himself covered. He gathered her close again, making a gruff noise as he ironed her onto his front with firm hands, like he wanted to absorb her right through his skin.

She couldn't help the greedy sobs that escaped her throat. She arched for maximum contact, few thoughts drifting in her head save for this being the most singularly exquisite experience of her life. When he kissed her again and rolled onto her, she made a noise of deep approval.

Then he was there, sliding deep into her, the sensation so sharp and strong she moaned into his mouth and wrapped her legs around his, holding him there so she could savor the connection.

They barely moved for a few minutes, just kissing and enjoying the union, looking into each other's eyes at one point to see the other's gaze was just as clouded with pleasure. More long, drugging kisses. Then, as if he knew something she didn't, he began to move.

"Oh." Sensations ebbed and flowed with his lovemaking, filling her with pleasure, drawing her tight with loss as he pulled away, then basking in the joy of his return. "Oh, Quincy." She couldn't hold back. Crisis rose inexorably and she was suddenly flying apart, shuddering in the arms that cradled her.

He slowed as her climax faded into soft pulses and rolled so they were side by side, still joined. He was still hard inside her.

"I wanted to do that together," she pouted, not really in a position to complain when she felt so danged good.

"I'm not ready for it to be over. Do you mind?" He rolled further, so he was on his back, pulling her atop him to stroke her back.

She made another satisfied noise as the movement stimulated where he still possessed her. With a luxurious movement on him, she admitted, "I don't mind one bit."

She felt like a femme fatale, a woman with the power to test a man's control. For the next few minutes, she controlled their lovemaking. She kissed him, had him at her mercy, and loved the way he watched her through slitted eyes, the way he reacted with tight noises of tested restraint.

It was an illusion, of course. The bolder she grew, the more aroused he became. He ran his hands over her with purpose, as deliberate in his attempts to provoke desire as she was. And when *he* was ready, he rolled her beneath him again.

"This time," he said through gritted teeth. "Together."

He moved with that powerful rhythm that had been her undoing the first time. This time, he was less reserved. She lost the last of her inhibitions and encouraged him. They bordered on aggressive so determined were they to meld into one being, but they were lost to the act, to each other.

When the peak arrived, they crested it with identical cries of joy and loss.

QUINCY WISHED HE'D thought to pick up something for dinner while he'd been out.

He wished he'd stayed with Nicki. Or talked her into staying here. Not to cook, although Quincy very much feared that, left to their own devices, this house of bachelors would rely on a steady diet of packaged foods.

No, he just wanted her to *be* here.

Where was she by now? He didn't know what time she finally drove away. He had left while she slept, leaving a note that had taken him way too long to draft. He'd wound up a few minutes late picking up his father and son after dithering over what to say. He still thought he'd revealed too much. Or not enough.

Wasn't sure I could leave if I woke you. Call me when you get to your dad's so I know you arrived safely. You're amazing. Q.

Had she been okay with waking to a note? Angry he hadn't said a proper goodbye? He really had struggled to force himself away from her after holding her for an hour while she slept.

Should he have asked her to stay? He kept thinking of her calling herself a failure. He couldn't stand between her and her dream. She deserved this chance to prove to herself she could succeed at acting. At anything.

They were very different personalities, too. They

couldn't work as a couple in the long run. Could they?

They had fit well in bed. She fit in his *life*, damn it. The house felt empty without her.

He bit back a curse, grabbed a lasagna from the freezer, and wanted to shove his head in the oven as he flicked it on. He wanted to cook out all these clashing thoughts.

Atlas came into the kitchen, a thankful distraction.

"Finished reading with Pops?" Quincy asked.

Atlas nodded.

"Can I do dis one now?" He held up a round piece of paper with crayon scribbles across it. It was the last paper ornament from the Advent calendar.

How did something so innocuous have the power to deliver such a heart punch?

"What does it says?" Atlas asked.

"What does it *say*," Quincy gently corrected, then read aloud, "Light a candle and say a prayer for all the moms in heaven." He stifled a sigh, thinking his emotions were a little too close to the surface for that one. He wanted to refuse out of self-preservation, but managed to find a compromise. "We'll get everything ready, but we'll do it later, after dinner, when it's time for bed."

Quincy moved one of the kitchen chairs to the sink and fetched the bag he had left in the pantry. Nicki always involved Atlas in the simplest of chores, and Quincy had begun to follow her example. His initial thought had been that it was quicker and easier to do things himself, but he was starting to see the value in keeping a kid busy and letting him learn how to turn on taps or hold a broom or pick up a towel and hang it on a rail.

Half the time it was a disaster, but Atlas had an inquisitive mind and an eagerness to learn. Quincy found it entertaining to watch his son experiment and try to master something.

In gathering the items for this activity, Quincy had to settle for a goldfish bowl from the pet store. He vaguely thought a fish might be a good starter pet, to see how they fared with one. Something to think about when Atlas's birthday rolled around.

Quincy gave the bowl a rinse, then set it in the sink, pointing to a random spot halfway up the side. "Fill it to here, but only use this tap. See the letter C? That means the water is cold." He pointed. "This one is hot. You could burn yourself. Don't touch that one."

"H. Hot." Atlas held his hands in the air like he was being robbed. "Don't touch."

"Nicki teach you that?" Quincy guessed with a private chuckle and a fresh pang of loss.

Atlas nodded and proceeded to test the different pressures of the cold tap while watching the bowl fill.

Tell him you love him.

He did love his son, Quincy recognized. Somehow, this wiry little bundle of curiosity had wormed into him in a way he didn't even understand, but what he felt was everything he understood love to be—loyalty and affection, trust and a desire to spend time with the little guy.

"When is Nicki comin' back?" Atlas asked with a swish-stop, swish-stop of the knob.

Quincy's thoughts stuttered with the run of water. "She had to go see her father for Christmas, remember? Then she's going away to work. You remember she told you that?"

Atlas nodded. Swish-stopped. Swish-stopped.

"But when is she comin' back? How many sweeps?"

"How many sleeps? Son—" A sense of foreboding came over him, making the words stick in his throat. He had to force them out. "She's not coming back. I thought you understood that."

Atlas stared up at him, water pouring in a steady stream. His face fell into anxious lines. His eyes filled to brimming pools. In a small voice, he asked, "Like Momma?"

Oh, hell. "No. Not like that—"

The bowl was overflowing. Quincy snapped off the water, but there was no stopping Atlas's breakdown. His chin crinkled, then his whole face screwed up. He clenched his eyes shut and tears squeezed out. As they began to roll down his face, his arms went straight. His mouth turned down before it opened in a wail of anguish loud enough to hurt Quincy's ears.

His cry penetrated like a knife all the way to Quincy's soul.

Quincy managed to bite back the curse that came to his

tongue, but he didn't know what to do. He started to reach for the boy, hesitated, then told himself not to be so damned scared of loving someone. It was hard for him, yes. He was out of practice, and he didn't know how to love *this* person.

But Atlas was broken. Inconsolable. And he was the boy's father.

He supposed he had expected rejection, but as he picked up the boy, Atlas wrapped his arms around Quincy's neck, buried his face in his throat, and cried so hard it scared him.

Atlas cried and cried.

Quincy's eyes stung. His heart cracked and expanded past its confines, wishing futilely that he could reach into the boy and fix his broken little heart. His arms ached where he held the boy's weight. His shoulders ached where he tried to hold back the world of hurt crushing his boy.

"It's okay, son. You have me. I love you." The first stammer of the statement felt awkward. Too honest. It was the realness that made it scary and hard. After that, though, it was easier. He set his cheek against the boy's hair and rocked him back and forth. "I know you miss her." It wasn't just Nicki he was missing. Quincy knew that. "I'm so sorry your momma is gone. But you have Pops and me. We both love you. So much."

He didn't try to tell Atlas to stop crying. It was long past time he let this out.

Hooking his foot on the chair leg, Quincy pulled it away from the sink, then sat and settled his son in his lap, keeping a tight hold on him, rubbing his back, hating this feeling of helplessness, but giving the boy's grief its due.

Eventually, Atlas wound down into small, shuddering breaths, arms still clinging around Quincy's neck. The fingers of one little hand flicked against his beard in a way that was odd and endearing. He kept up the movement like it was a comfort action, petting the corner of his father's jaw while he grew heavier and quieter until he stilled. Quincy realized the boy had fallen asleep.

He started to carry him upstairs, but Pops saw them and frowned with concern. "Sick?"

"No, just—" Quincy looked into his son's tearstained face. "I've screwed up, Pops. Big time. Having Nicki here… He fell in love with her." The weight of that was so much heavier than the boy's slight weight in his arms. "Now he's not just missing Karen. He's going to grow up thinking all women leave."

Pops set a heavy hand on his shoulder and gave him the man-to-man stare, even though he was a good half a foot shorter than Quincy.

"Son, if I gave you a list of all the times I felt like I failed you, you'd wonder why social services hadn't been a regular part of our lives. Having Nicki here was the best thing that could have happened for you and Atlas." He smiled indulgently at the way Quincy cradled the boy so lovingly. "The only mistake you're making is letting her go."

"She's *gone*," he said helplessly, turning away to start up the stairs.

He had failed to tell her he loved her, so she left.

The words had been too big, too close to the bone. Of course she wouldn't stay if he only wanted to *see* if they could fall in love. She might have stayed, though, if he had told her he was already there.

With a shaken breath, he sat down on Atlas's bed, tucked his stuffed dog against the boy's chest, then snugged his son closer into his own chest, like a teddy bear from which he could find comfort for his own loss.

SO MUCH FOR an early start. It was almost five o'clock before Nicki got away after waking alone. That had stung, but at least Quincy left a note. Not a love note, but one that said she was amazing. He had asked her to call when she got to her dad's.

She was fighting tears as she made her way out of Marietta. Had she really expected more after they made love? A grand gesture? A declaration that he couldn't live without her? She understood enough about Quincy to know he didn't do things like that. Talking wasn't his forte.

Meanwhile, her forte was being rejected, so she got pretty much what she expected. Good thing she was going back to acting because she was as much a failure as a nursing aide, falling in love with her boss, then crashing and burning at *that*—

Oh, damn, she couldn't see the road. She pulled over and dug through her mess of stuff for the crumpled box of tissue buried on the floor of the passenger side. Her foot slipped off the clutch. Her car lurched and stalled.

Par for the course. She snapped off the radio, not in the mood for Pentatonix, even though "Mary Did You Know" was one of her favorites. She blew her nose and mopped up her cheeks, but the tears kept leaking out.

Failure, failure, *sniff*, failure. Outside, a few tiny flakes drifted down while she sat on that lonely stretch of road and threw the biggest pity party no one was around to see.

She didn't want to leave Marietta. Nothing about what awaited her in Texas made her excited. She did want to see her dad, she allowed. Spending time with the Ryans had reminded her that her time with her own father was finite. His health was good, but no one lived forever. She should stop taking him for granted.

Sniff.

But what about the acting job? Yes, it was a good one, but it was one job. One that would last a few years if she was very lucky, then she would be back to auditioning. She had said, "Yes," to salvage her tattered ego. Maybe she was still trying to say, "*See?*" to Gloria.

For heaven's sake, *why*? Because she had never forgiven the woman for not being her mother? For trying to keep her from leaving Glacier Creek? For trying to protect her from battering herself nearly to death against a high, hard wall?

What a crime! How dare she?

Sniff.

Nicki didn't want to go to Texas and pretend to be someone's wife and mother. She didn't want to chase some old ambition that had been motivated by a need to escape deep sadness. She was sad now, and she was doing it to herself, inflicting loss on herself because she was afraid Quincy didn't really want her to be his wife and the mother of his child.

Children?

Sob.

Being a stepmom used to be her idea of hell. Now she thought it would be such an honor if he would let her have a place in Atlas's life.

So why was she leaving? Because he hadn't *begged* her to stay?

She pulled out his note from where she had tucked it in her bra, against her skin. *You're amazing.*

She'd spent years being told she was too dark, but couldn't carry off blond. She was pretty, but not as pretty as her headshot. Her brown eyes made her look ethnic, but not ethnic *enough*. She was too tall, too heavy, not chesty enough, maybe if she could sing… Did she want to do nude scenes? Because that opened doors…

Quincy didn't criticize her. The only thing he had ever tried to change about her was telling her not to call herself a failure.

The words he had written, the way he had made love to her, even the way he came to say a private goodbye… Those *were* his version of a grand gesture.

And his actions? She was a student of human behavior. The way he had acted toward her, most especially today when he refused to make her choose between her career and him, that told her louder than words he genuinely cared for her well-being. In the same way he wanted what was best for his son, he wanted the best for her.

She was so used to being rejected, she'd seen Quincy as another broken dream waiting to happen. He hadn't *told* her to go. In fact, he had said he would like her to stay, but that he wouldn't *ask* her to.

He didn't want to make her choose.

Holding the steering wheel, she tipped her head back and groaned at the ceiling.

Quincy understood that walking away from acting had to be her choice, but she had made that choice last year, when she went back to school. Yes, she'd done it with a certain wistfulness, wishing she had at least landed one really great role before she gave up, but guess what? She *had* landed that role.

She didn't have to spend a year in Texas to bask in the accomplishment of being *cast*. She would always have the knowledge that she had measured up. She could easily move on to making a life with Quincy without regret for what might have been.

Poignant sweetness expanded in her. A sense of peace with her past and optimism for her future.

She reached to turn the key, eager to go back and tell him she would look for work in Marietta. They could see what happened. She wouldn't regret staying either way.

Her car made one coughing noise, then sputtered into nothing, refusing to turn over.

QUINCY WAS KEEPING his phone handy, waiting for a text or call from Nicki. She would be out of range for a lot of the mountain driving. It would probably be hours yet, so he wasn't exactly concerned by the silence, but he wanted to hear from her.

He shouldn't have let her leave without telling her he loved her. If anything happened, he would never forgive himself.

They were about to sit down to dinner when his phone buzzed and her name came up. He found himself fumbling it. "Hello?"

"It's me." She was breathing as though walking briskly. "I'm not at my dad's. My stupid car broke down again."

"*Where?*" He rose and hurried to the back door, taking his keys off the hook as he scuffed into his shoes.

"Just outside Marietta. I wound up having a bite with the Tierneys before I left, so I was barely past town limits, thank goodness. But I didn't want you worrying that you hadn't heard from me—"

"Where *exactly?* I'm coming to get you."

"Quincy, I'm fine. It's not that cold. It's actually kind of peaceful. I've left a message for the Tierneys. I'm sure they'll let me use the flat again tonight, but if not, I'll go to one of the hotels."

"You're not getting a hotel. Are you kidding me? I'm coming to get you." He motioned to his father to start eating without him. "Where are you? I'll be there as soon as I can."

SHE WAS RELIEVED to see him. She hadn't wanted to leave her laptop in the car, dinosaur that it was, so she was carrying that with a change of clothes and her purse. It was a heavy load.

Nevertheless, she claimed, "You really didn't have to do this," as they stood at the back of the SUV, stowing her things.

"Of course I did. You're not going to a hotel, either." He slammed the back and came with her to her door.

"I don't want to impose—"

He paused in opening the door for her.

"Are you serious?" He looked baffled, more than a little impatient with her, but his gaze was grave as he searched her expression. "Do you remember where we were this afternoon? I've been kicking myself for not—Damn it. I *love* you, Nicki. It scares the hell out of me, but I do. And I sure as hell am not about to leave the woman I love by the side of the road on Christmas Eve."

She wanted to admonish him for swearing, tease him and ask about other days of the year, but all she could do was stand there and tear up afresh. She touched her mouth as it formed a soft, "Oh."

"Am I reading things wrong?"

"No. I mean, I hoped that you felt... Oh, Quincy!" She threw herself into his arms. "I love you so much!"

He muttered something that might have been, "Thank God," as he closed his arms tight around her. "We'll figure something out," he promised. "Long distance isn't great, but—"

"No, I was coming back." She pulled back to set her feet fully on the ground. "I've decided not to go. I'll find a job in Marietta. We can date and see what happens—No?"

He shook his head, making her heart stop and drop.

He hugged her again, hard, then let her feet touch ground again. "You really want to stay?"

"Yes." She said it firmly, without any doubt.

"Then can't we just get married?" His hand went into his hair. "That was a terrible proposal. But I want you in my house, Nicki. Every night when you leave, I'm disappointed. In the morning, I'm waiting for you to come back. If you don't want to live with Pops, I get it. We can find our own place, but spending time with Atlas is how I began to feel like a father. I want to live with you, so we'll become a husband and wife. I want us to be a family."

Her breath thinned out like smoke that dissipated until it was gone. Her smile wobbled.

"That was actually a really good proposal." She blinked, trying to catch back the happy tears forming in her eyes, barely able to speak. "I want that, too."

She stepped into him. When she turned up her face to kiss him, tiny flakes of snow floated in the glowing light above his dark hair, turning the moment fairy tale perfect. "I love you."

"I love you, too."

Christmas Day

"Mmm," a male growl sounded against her neck and firm arms hugged her naked back into his naked front. "You *are* here. I was afraid it was a dream."

She smiled sleepily, not even opening her eyes, but whispered the incantation that only came once a year. "It's Christmas."

Behind her, she felt Quincy lift his head to look at the clock. "Is he up? Or can we steal some adult time?"

Maury and Atlas had been thrilled to see her come in with Quincy last night. Maury went over the moon when Quincy told him they were engaged. Atlas had hugged her and stuck pretty close the rest of the evening, sitting in her lap as they lit the candles in the bowl, then asking her to read to him at bedtime. He had gone to bed later than usual, but slept solid.

An hour later, they heard him stirring and pulled their satiated bodies from the covers, smiling lazily at each other as they dressed. Her heart was so full she could hardly bear it.

"They stiw goin'," Atlas said as they went downstairs and

found the four candles in the globe still floating and burning.

Nicki took it as a sign that they were all being blessed by their mommas, her decision to stay with Quincy especially. Her father had passed along a similar blessing last night, when she had called to tell him she was staying in Marietta for the night and why. They were all going to drive down tomorrow for a proper introduction and visit.

As Maury ambled down the stairs, Atlas went to the Advent calendar and pointed out there were no more spots to fill.

"It's Kwissmass! Cahr-ismas." He corrected himself, trying hard to get the R sound, but he was too excited after that. "We can open da pwesents!"

Nicki laughed with equal excitement, delighted to see how big he smiled and how bright his eyes shone. "Stockings first. That was always our tradition." She glanced at Quincy.

"Us, too," he confirmed, then caught her hand, tugging her down beside him on the sofa, pulling her in close against his side. "You're the best present I could have this morning, you know that?" he said into her hair.

"You, too." She gave his beard a little rub with the tip of her nose. She didn't care one iota that there was nothing under the tree for her.

"But what's this?" Maury said as he helped Atlas take the stockings off their hooks. "Looks like Santa brought you something, Nicki. Forgot to put your name on it, but at least he found you. He's a clever one, that ol' St. Nick."

He handed a gray woolen sock with white trim to Atlas and told the boy to give it to her.

"Thank you," she said, wanting to make a joke about seeing Maury buy these socks a week ago, but not wanting to spoil the magic for Atlas.

"What could it be?" she murmured, glancing at Quincy for a clue.

He shrugged in the most painfully nonchalant way while Atlas said, "Open an' see," making them all smile at his earnest answer.

"Well, um, *Santa*." She glanced between the men. "Thank you. I didn't expect this."

Atlas attacked the contents of his stocking with enthusiasm, making excited noises of discovery as he revealed little building block kits and action figurines.

Both men ignored their own stockings in favor of watching her, making her all the more self-conscious. Nicki dug for the one item. It was a velvet box.

Seriously? The stores wouldn't have been open.

She drew out the indigo-colored jeweler's box with the gold-embossed marking. Something about it struck her as old fashioned, but quality. Little trembles took over her nerve endings.

As she licked her lips and told herself it was probably earrings, Quincy slid off the sofa beside her and onto one knee.

She dropped the little box into her lap and clapped her hands over her mouth. Then moved them to her hot cheeks and was tempted to hide her dampening eyes. Her heart took off in a race inside her chest.

"Nicole Darren…" His voice was so strong yet tender, deep and sincere.

"Oh, Quincy." Her eyes filled so fast they stung. Her mouth began to tug every which way, wanting to smile, but emotion made her lips quiver. "How—?"

She could barely hear him as he continued speaking, sounding equally overcome.

"It was my mother's. Pops gave it to me last night, while you were reading with Atlas." He opened the little box to reveal a princess-cut solitaire in a yellow-gold setting. It was simple and pretty and now she couldn't see it because her vision had completely blurred.

"I mean all of this." She pressed her hands to cheeks that were hot and round with her huge smile. "I love you so much, all of you. How am I this happy? How is this so perfect?"

"It's Christmas."

Of course. The obvious answer. They both laughed.

"Will you marry me, Nicki?"

"I would be so honored, Quincy. Yes," she managed in a trembling voice. Then sniffed and had to wipe the tears that were dripping down her cheeks.

Maury chuckled and reached out with a clean handkerchief. "I brought this down thinking we might need it."

Nicki laughed through her tears, gulping back her sniffles

as Quincy slid the ring onto her finger. It was a tiny bit loose, but she would put a bit of tape on it until they could get it sized. No way was she *not* wearing it today. Christmas Day. The day he proposed. She had never been so happy in her life.

"I'll ask your father for permission when we see him," Quincy said.

"He'll love that." She hooked her arms around his neck and leaned to kiss him.

They kept it chaste, on account of their audience, but held onto each other for an extra second, trying to pull themselves together.

Atlas, caught up in his own special day, unwrapped the tear-off calendar she had put in his stocking. "What's diss?"

It was the distraction they needed.

"That's so you can learn to read. Each day has a word." She helped him turn it over. "See. January First says, 'Pop!—goes the fireworks. It's a New Year!'"

Atlas ran his finger under the words, repeating carefully, "Pops goes da fi-ahhrr wahhrrks."

"Not *Pops*—" Nicki teased.

They all laughed, even Atlas, proving there was a sharp sense of humor under that quiet exterior.

The calendar was discarded, and Nicki picked it up. "It's a little advanced for him, but he seemed to like the countdown of the Advent calendar," she said in an aside to Quincy.

"Were we counting down? I think I was counting up. Twenty-five of the best days of my life." He sat beside her again and centered the ring on her finger. "Christmas elf," he murmured. "More like my Christmas miracle."

"Aw." She smiled, deeply touched.

"I mean it." He brought her hand to his mouth and kissed her knuckle. "I'm looking forward to spending the rest of the year with you. All the rest of the years of my life."

"Me, too. Merry Christmas."

December 14th, Two Years Later

"Hey, babe?" Quincy called as he came up the stairs. "That was Joan on the phone. She said she and Dad are at the church. The nativity thing is going to start soon. Are you almost ready?"

Nicki flung open the door to their small en-suite bathroom and gave her husband a helpless look. He wore his winter jacket and held his phone. His eyes widened when he saw she wore a towel and wet hair. Her face was rinsed clean of the makeup she had applied an hour ago.

"Small change of plans. We're staging our own nativity play. My water just broke."

"Are you serious? I—" He took a step toward her, then backed out of the room to look down the stairs. He lifted his phone, started to swear, bit it back, sent her a dumbfounded look, then called, "Atlas!"

The boy charged up the stairs wearing his own jacket and a woolen hat. "Are we going? What's wrong?"

"You have to stay with Pops and Grandma Joan tonight," Quincy said, plainly trying to grasp order out of chaos. "Mom says the baby is coming. I have to take her to the hospital."

Atlas blinked bewildered eyes at her. "You said the baby would come after Christmas."

"That's what the doctor told me, but babies are pretty notorious for not looking at calendars." She wrinkled her nose at him, trying to ignore the small contraction working its way across her back. "Can you go find pajamas and pack clothes for two nights into your school bag? I'll help soon as I'm dressed."

"I got it," Quincy said in the easy, tag-team rapport they had developed even before they admitted they had feelings for one another. "Do you have your own bag packed?"

"I was going to do it this weekend." She opened a drawer and pulled out clothes to wear to the hospital. "Once December hit, I got so caught up in Christmas I let all the baby prep slide… I kept thinking I would be overdue and have time after Christmas to organize everything."

To her husband's credit, he did *not* say, "I told you so," even though he had asked a few times about whether he should assemble the change table and whether she had pre-registered at the hospital.

She sighed, overwhelmed as she realized how much she *hadn't* done.

He came across and took her into a comforting embrace. "You okay?"

"A little bit freaked out," she admitted, resting her wet

head against his jacket. "But it's only two weeks early."

"I'll be with you the whole time." He kissed her forehead. "I love you."

"I love you, too." Her husband had been her rock through two years of changes. After they married, she had taken a part-time job in Marietta and went through the process to adopt Atlas. Quincy had kept his travel to a minimum, so they could give Atlas all the support he needed as he started school and speech therapy—both of which had been a rousing success. Maury had also married and moved with Joan into a nice apartment in town, making room in the house for Quincy and Nicki to grow their family.

They increased it by one girl, they discovered twelve hours later.

"I know we talked about your mom's name or mine if we had a girl," Nicki said as they gazed at her tiny, perfect little face, finally alone in their private room after a textbook delivery. "But yesterday, Atlas said he liked the name Natalie. I looked it up. It means, 'Born at Christmas.' That's ten days away, but—"

"I love it." Quincy dragged his wonder-filled eyes from their daughter to hers. "She obviously didn't want to wait a year to have Christmas with us. She wants to be part of it now. Yes. Natalie. What time is it? I want to phone Atlas and tell him."

He patted his pockets, then went to find his jacket where he fished out his phone and placed a face call. "Hey, Pops, is

Atlas up?"

Maury called Atlas over to look into the screen. Atlas was still rubbing the sleep from his eyes as he leaned into his grandfather. "Hi, Dad."

"Hey, champ. Guess what you got for Christmas? A sister. This is Natalie." He showed his son their newborn.

"Yessss!" Atlas high-fived with Pops.

"You're happy we're using your name?" Quincy guessed dryly.

"I'm happy I have a sister."

"Oh." He exchanged a how-about-that look with Nicki.

"How's Nicki? When can we come to the hospital?" Pops asked.

"Both are doing great. We're going to see if we can sleep, but everything went really well. They might be discharged later today. Let me call you back in a few hours."

"Hmph. Not the way it was done when you were born, but okay. We'll be home all day. You let me know."

Quincy ended the call and scratched his cheek. "I was never going to be this guy. A *dad*. Having a son was a shock. Now I have a daughter, and I'm so delighted to have *two* kids… Is it too soon to talk about another one?"

"Way too soon," she assured him, making him chuckle.

"I was joking." He cradled her jaw as he looked into her eyes. "Mostly. I am happy. And grateful." His expression grew reflective and sincere. "I don't say that enough, but I am incredibly grateful to you, Nicki. Making a baby is not the accomplishment. You helped me become a father in the way that matters most. I love you so very much for that."

"You had good genes," she tried to say dismissively, but she teared up. "And you're the best father I could imagine for my children. I have never once regretted not going to Texas. I want to be here, with you, every single day."

They kissed, and it was filled with celebration and gratitude, sweet passion, and renewal of vows. It brimmed with love. Lots and lots of love.

The End

Dear Reader,

I hope you enjoyed HIS CHRISTMAS MIRACLE. Would you like to make a calendar similar to the one Nicki made for Quincy and Atlas? I've designed a printable Advent calendar with suggested activities that you can print, color, and customize for your little elves. Download the file here: danicollins.com/download/405930003

It's my gift to you and you *must* open it before Christmas!

Enjoy the season,
Dani

Enjoy USA Today Bestselling Author
Dani Collins' new series…

Love in Montana

Book 1: **Hometown Hero**
Skye and Chase's story

Book 2: **Blame the Mistletoe**
Liz and Blake's story

Book 3: **The Bachelor's Baby**
Meg and Linc's story

Book 4: **His Blushing Bride**
Piper and Bastian's story

Book 5: **His Christmas Miracle**
Nicki and Quincy's story

Available at your favorite online retailer!

About the Author

After twenty-five years of writing and submitting, **Dani Collins** won the 2013 Reviewer's Choice Award for Best First In Series from Romantic Times Book Reviews. Known mostly for her emotional, passionate Harlequin Presents, she has also published a hilarious romantic comedy, an epic medieval fantasy romance, and a pair of extremely erotic erotic romances. Dani writes anything, so long as it's romance.

Thank you for reading

His Christmas Miracle

If you enjoyed this book, you can find more from all our great authors at TulePublishing.com, or from your favorite online retailer.

Made in the USA
Charleston, SC
14 November 2016